THE BOOK OF LIVING and DYING

NATALE GHENT

THE BOOK OF LIVING AND DYING

Harper*Trophy*Canada™
An imprint of HarperCollins*PublishersLtd*

Published by Harper*Trophy*Canada™, an
imprint of HarperCollins Publishers Ltd

First edition

HarperCollins books may be purchased for
educational, business, or sales promotional
use through our Special Markets Department.

HarperCollins Publishers Ltd
2 Bloor Street East, 20th Floor
Toronto, Ontario, Canada
M4W 1A8

www.harpercollins.ca

Library and Archives Canada Cataloguing
in Publication

Ghent, Natale, 1962–
The book of living and dying / Natale
Ghent. – 1st ed.

ISBN-13: 978-0-00-639349-8
ISBN-10: 0-00-639349-7

I. Title.

PS8563.H46B66 2005   C813'.6
C2004-907309-5

HC 9 8 7 6 5 4 3 2 1

Printed and bound in the United States

For Mark, who burned so brightly,
And for Jasmine, who shines on

chapter one

Sarah Wagner had known all night that something was coming. There was the warning of the black locust branches tapping urgently against the window. And the street lamp flaring and exploding in a shower of phosphorous crystals and glass. She had been restless, too, the sweat beading above her lip, the floorboards creaking like footsteps as she struggled to find a comfortable position in bed. No matter how she tried, she couldn't shake the sensation of being watched, or the barely perceptible feeling that someone—or something—was holding her hand.

She smelled him before she saw him. The odour of earth and rain arriving moments before he appeared beside the bed, boots glistening with mud. Funny how she noticed his boots, despite the blood pounding in her temples. But it was his face that shocked her the most—shining and slightly flushed, like he'd just been running in the rain. Like he'd never been sick at all. Her heart pumped in her throat as he reached for her, his mouth swinging open and closed like the loosely hinged gate to a dark and deadly garden. She tried to scream when his cold hand encircled her wrist, but

1

could only gape helplessly back at him, the darkness spilling from his lips and flooding into her brain.

"*Please go away,*" she whispered.

* * *

Sarah stared out the window. The sugar maples blazed crimson against a concrete sky. Fall was her favourite time of year. It was bold and unforgiving. No apologies, no half-cloaked secrets like hushed voices in hospital rooms. She loved everything about it—except school. It was only the first week and already she was bored. Senior year. How had she made it this far?

It certainly wasn't the other students who'd helped her through. The petty politics of high school—she was sick of it. Dates with "A-list" boys she didn't even like. Running with frivolous groups of girls. Better to belong than to not belong. She'd had her hand in it: the gossip, the back-stabbing. How empty it all was. How hollow it had all seemed in the face of his despair. So she'd just stopped. Stopped hanging out. Stopped making herself available. Stopped answering the phone. Drifting away had proved easier than maintaining ties. Boys lost interest quickly. Friends fell away like chaff. Except Donna, the self-professed outcast. To her, pretty much everyone else was stupid or boring or a waste of time. And there was Peter, as well. She couldn't seem to get rid of him.

Sarah rubbed her eyes with her fingers. The dull throb of a burgeoning headache pulsed along her brow. Pressing the heels of her hands against her eyelids, she increased the

2

pressure to the point of pain, then released, sending pin-points of light exploding across the dark screen in her head. It would get worse before the day was through, she knew. That was the pattern. She checked her shirt pocket for aspirin but found a pack of Juicy Fruit gum instead. The wrapper shone brightly as she extracted a piece, opening it carefully so as not to tear the paper, removing the gum, refolding the silver liner, then sliding it neatly into its cover so that it looked like it hadn't been opened. She'd done this out of habit since she was a kid. A trap for her mother or her brother.

The gum felt powdery against her tongue. Sarah exam-ined the package. *"You want, you need, you gotta have more sweet!"* Chewing gum was the only thing that kept her from coming completely unglued in class. Kept her mind from slipping loose and spilling over her desk. She imagined the inside of her skull, brains held together with strings of gum like rubbery webs. She chewed lots of it, sometimes several packs a day. Calculus was the worst. It took a whole pack to get through that class alone. When she was little, she used to swallow her gum instead of spitting it out when it lost its flavour. Before her brother told her it would stick—a big ball of gum growing in her stomach—and she would die. So she'd quit doing it, then worried endlessly about the gum she had already swallowed.

But it was John who had died. The brave one, the gifted one, the prodigal son. With his music and his dreams. Strik-ing out in the world, free from the stultifying shame her fam-ily served up as the house specialty. He was going to rescue her. "We'll live together," he had said. She could be his roadie, travelling with the band, waking up in a different place every day. She loved the idea of being with him, of being part of something bigger and, most of all, of being as far away from her mother's disapproval as possible. She was a cold woman, an emotional iceberg. "The ice queen," Sarah called her in kinder moments. But to make matters worse, she was weak. Beneath her frigid exterior was a mewling child, convinced that John's sickness was somehow a judgment against her. It wasn't long before Sarah stopped trying to please her altogether. She was only thirteen when she made the conscious decision to avoid her instead, wagering the bulk of her carefully guarded dreams on John. He was going to come get her the day she turned eighteen—he'd promised.

It was the illness that wore his promise away, drop by drop. Her love had been helpless against the glistening line of circumstance, hope reeled from the turbulent waters of her heart to thump gasping against the cold stone of fact: He was dying. He was dead. It had surprised Sarah—surprised everyone—how he struggled to hold on to such a small corner of life, kicking and moaning with the determination of a newborn. Why he wouldn't just let go and be rid of it, the dreariness, the pain. He said, *"I'm so scared."*

Fall always reminded her of him. He'd left by degrees, like the leaves, until only the bones were left, the fire of him blown gradually away with the advancing cold. Until everything was gone. Except the rain. And the photos, cluttering up the house, collecting in corners and the backs of drawers in small piles. Her mother was numb, absent. Refused to talk about it. Sarah became methodical, gathering the photos and pressing them carefully into books, adding whatever notation she could remember. *Summer, '91. Grandma's backyard. Christmas, '95. Uncle Fred's place.* When she couldn't remember she would write the names of the people on the back of the photos with a question mark. This

4

seemed fitting. Wasn't that all anyone left behind? A name and a question with no answer?

An image of John standing beside the bed entered her mind, sending a shiver up her spine. The shock of seeing his face. Why had he come back? She touched her wrist where his hand had been and couldn't help but feel that she was somehow responsible. It was possible to admit now, after the fact, that there were times when the weight of his illness had been too much for her, when the oppressive days of sickness had made her want to scream or run away and she'd found herself secretly wishing for a quicker end, then frantically retracting such wicked thoughts in horrified remorse. Or the times when she would drag her feet and arrive later at the hospital than she had said she would, to find him waiting angrily, seething with unspoken reproach. He had become so hateful near the end, too, as though he could see the betrayal in her heart, his personality eroding over the weeks until suspicion and morphine consumed his true self. It wasn't his fault, she'd tell herself when he would bark at her over the simplest things, like forgetting that he took only ice chips—no water—or that he liked his pillow at a certain angle. It was as if he blamed her—blamed everyone for what had happened to him. And she blamed herself as well. She had failed him. Was that why he had come back? Out of anger? What was it that he had tried to say before she had wished him away?

The wind wailed, rattling its fists against the windows. A discarded juice carton tumbled and bounced across the parking lot, coming to a stop against the wire fence that surrounded the school. *Keeping the kids in or out?* Sarah let her eyes relax until the honeycomb of wire fence blurred into a solid wall of grey.

It was a good thing her dad had died before John did. It would have only made things worse to have him there, wrestling with his anguish over losing his only son, fighting violently with her mother, drowning a slow suicide in cheap scotch whisky. Sarah could hear the nurse's voice over the phone like it was yesterday, a heavy Southern accent drawling like tupelo honey from the spoon. "A-neur-y-sm." But death had been thankfully fast for Mr. Wagner. Joking with hospital staff one minute, flinging backwards onto the bed the next—one hand clutching his chest. Of course that last part Sarah only imagined. She couldn't know for sure. But one thing she did know was that he'd been alone, as always, on the road in some strange place, away from his family. A drifter, a snake oil salesman, cruising into town to sell sewing machines to bored housewives with bad hair and too much lipstick. Pathetic.

Sarah shifted in her seat. She could feel the weight of his stare, the guy who sat against the wall, three seats back. Following the line of her cheek, the landscape of her breasts beneath her sweater, her hips curving inside her jeans. Surveying. Making maps. Turning from the window, she met his gaze and forced him to avert his eyes, then looked over at Donna, whose black rag doll hair framed her small angry face. Donna raised her eyebrows impudently and flipped her middle finger from behind her calculus book toward their teacher, Mr. Kovski, with his side-swept hair and synthetic brown leisure suit from the seventies. Sarah laughed. Mr. Kovski paused, then continued to drone until the bell rang, calling out some last-minute homework assignment as the students bustled out of the classroom.

"What's his problem?" Donna asked as they jostled with the other students in the hall.

"I guess he just loves calculus."

"Not him. That other creep. Michael what's-his-name. The new greaseball who keeps staring at you in class." Donna stopped in front of her locker, dropping her books in a loud heap on the floor. Turning her combination quickly, she yanked violently on the lock, then slammed her hand against the locker door when it wouldn't open.

Sarah sighed. "Turn it slower." Her own lock opened easily, the chrome dial cool between her fingers, the neat click of the mechanism sounding as it yielded to her touch. A quick tug on the locker door revealed her own books stacked with library precision, the familiar bottle of aspirin to one side. Extra-strength, coated capsules. Sarah popped the bottle cap and shook a couple of tablets into her hand, pushed them into her mouth and swallowed. No water needed. Affixed with grey duct tape to her locker door was a small, pink plastic-framed mirror. She checked her reflection. Pale blue eyes, even paler skin, a slight pout to her mouth. Her hair long and curly and brown—nothing like the straight hair that she wanted so badly, the kind all the girls had in the magazines. But her eyes—she wouldn't trade those for anything. They were exactly like John's: large and blue and a little bit sad. Should she tell Donna about seeing him? She needed to talk to somebody about it, to draw the curtain of fear in her heart and let some light in. But Donna was in a mood today.

"Mort," Sarah said. "His last name is Mort."

Donna scoffed dismissively. "Sounds like a geek."

"It's his last name, Donna. It's not his fault. He's not so bad."

"Not so bad? The guy's a creepy wanker! What is wrong with you, Wagner? It isn't normal to go around staring at people like that."

Sarah shrugged.

Donna wrenched her locker door open with a metallic crash. Sid Vicious sneered from a Sex Pistols poster inside. "Don't you know what guys like that do? They stare at you all day in school then go home and pull themselves in the privacy of their parents' bathroom."

"God, Donna!"

"It's true."

"Come on. He's just a guy."

"He's a creepy masturbating geek." She made a jerking motion with her hand.

"You don't even know him."

"I know his type."

Sarah clucked disdainfully. "His type. He's been at our school for less than a week and you've got him pegged. What is your issue with him?"

There was a fleeting look in Donna's eyes, as though she was about to disclose a secret, but it vanished quickly as she stepped back in exaggerated revelation. "Oh my God, you like him!"

"I do not!"

"You like Mortimer."

"I just don't think he's that bad, that's all. He seems pretty smart."

"Why? Because of his long hair and the Dead Kennedys T-shirt that he wears like a uniform?"

"I would have thought that you'd like that."

Donna kicked her books into her locker. "Retro crap. He probably bought the shirt at some stupid fringe shop or something. I bet he's never even listened to their music. I heard his dad's a prof or something."

"Who cares if his dad's a prof?" Sarah said, shooting

Donna a look of disgust. "He's in my media arts class. He seems to know a lot of stuff."

"So that makes him okay?" Donna sucked in her bottom lip and nodded smugly. "God, you're such a pushover, Wagner. Just wait until he starts stalking you." She leaned toward Sarah and moaned.

"Shut up, Donna! He's coming over here."

Donna moaned louder. Sarah hid her face in her locker. "You idiot," she said, laughing into her jacket so she wouldn't have to see his face.

As Michael walked by, Donna began to pogo up and down, yelling out the lyrics to the Buzzcocks' "Orgasm Addict."

"Okay. I get it!" Sarah whispered angrily, clamping a hand over her friend's mouth. "He's a creepy masturbating geek. Satisfied?"

Donna shook her head and burst out laughing. "I don't care if you love Mortimer as long as you still love me."

"You know I'll always love you," Sarah said. "Just don't bug me today, okay? I'm feeling sensitive."

"Oooo, sensitive . . ." Donna put her arm around Sarah's shoulder. "Come on. Let's go to the Queen's for a cup of j."

"Can't. I have band practice."

"*I have band practice*," Donna mimicked her. "When are you going to quit that stupid band and join a real group? You're a rock 'n' roll goddess, Wagner. Live the dream."

Sarah ignored her, pulling the guitar case from her locker. Shutting the door, she engaged the lock, testing it to make sure it was secure. "See ya," she said, turning away.

"Hey! I'll buy!" Donna called after her, but Sarah only waved over her shoulder and disappeared down the crowded hall.

* * *

She was the first to arrive in the music room. Closing the door, Sarah shut out the voices and noise from the hall. She placed the guitar on top of a table, the worn black case covered in stickers. New York, Boston, Chicago—a sticker for every city John had gigged in. Forty-four in total. Two for Chicago, his favourite place. There was a sticker of the Chicago flag right in the middle of the case. He had wanted to be buried with that flag draped over his coffin, military style. A soldier of the blues. But they hadn't buried him that way. She'd forgotten about the flag in the end. Fear tugged with quick fingers at the back of her neck as the spectre of John shot into her mind again. Sarah forced the image from her head, ran her hands over the guitar case and opened the latches with two low thuds.

The smell of wood and polish drifted into the room. Fender Stratocaster. Tobacco Sunburst. His first love. The guitar gleamed as though bewitched, the light trembling like a lover's hand across the varnish. Sarah touched the neck, the finish worn dull from John's fingers. He'd driven a cab for months to pay for the guitar, bumming money from friends for the deposit. The guy at the hockshop had demanded half the price upfront. John hated driving that cab but he had to have the guitar. He grew a beard, let his hair go wild and wore a black leather jacket with the collar upturned to protect his neck, just in case anyone got any ideas about stabbing him. That happened all the time in Chicago, he told her. "Some rubbie jonesin' for a hit, looking for easy money."

Lifting the guitar from its case, Sarah attached the strap to one end, and then the other, the way she'd seen John do it. She let it hang, feeling the familiar weight of it across her shoulder, the body resting low against her legs. It had felt so heavy the first time she'd held it. Now it seemed comfortable and easy to carry. Pushing the jack into the amplifier, she smiled when she heard the hum and snap of electricity. She strummed a chord tentatively. Her fingers were stiff and clumsy, compared to John's. Adjusting the knobs, she strummed again until she was satisfied with the sound. Peter and the other band members eventually burst into the room, their high spirits and loud voices shattering her solitude.

* * *

The school was all but empty by the time Sarah left; her footsteps echoed lightly down the hall. She could hear Peter turning the key to lock the music room door on the second floor. Afraid he would try to ask her out again, she hurried to get out of the building. He was always looking for opportunities to catch her alone. It wasn't that she didn't like him. She'd given him a chance—once. He just wasn't her type after all. He didn't do anything for her. She was fine going back to being just friends. That's all she wanted. She'd run these reasons over and over in her head, but no matter how many times she examined the situation, she couldn't find a way to save the patient, to tell the truth without killing his ego. So she took to avoiding him when she was by herself. She was running out of excuses.

Peter was calling her name, his feet scuffling quickly down the stairs to catch up with her. The metal bar on the school door gave a loud clunk as she pushed it and slipped with John's guitar into the night. The air was cool and tingling with needles of rain atomized to a fine mist. Sarah checked the road for cars before crossing, even though she knew the streets would be deserted. There was no life after dark in Terrace, Massachusetts.

As Sarah stepped from the curb, an exquisite rust-coloured leaf floated down, illuminated by the streetlights. It lifted on the wind and danced invitingly in front of her like a small kite. *Quercus alba.* "White oak," she said to herself. She had learned the Latin names from one of her teachers at school, the foreign sound of the words soothing her when she couldn't sleep after the sickness came. She had books at home, books she had made herself, cataloguing the leaves and the names of the trees that had released them, their varied personalities, the subtleties of design, the details. She had focused her mind and discovered a whole world that she had never considered before, opening up, calling her in. It gave her a sense of belonging when everything else had abandoned her—including her mother, who didn't seem to care what she did any more. Didn't care about her marks in school or who she hung around with or how late she stayed out—or if she even came home at all. Her mother didn't care about anything, it seemed, except coffee and cigarettes.

The ethereal leaf dipped and bobbed. Sarah followed as it floated toward the library, pulsing lightly, like a butterfly, only to flutter away again as she went to catch it. Twirling in the air, the leaf slipped behind the wall of the library and was gone. The wall stood in shadow. Just the kind of place a ghost would like to haunt. "Don't be silly," Sarah muttered. Taking a sharp breath, she walked quickly around the corner and then stopped, peering through the dark. Was that the leaf, just under the bushes? The moisture dripped off the cedars as she knelt on the ground, stretching out her hand. She turned her head slightly to increase her reach and caught the figure of a man watching her from the shadows.

Sarah shouted as she fell back, one arm clutching the guitar, heels skidding against the wet grass. Trying to right herself so she could run, she recognized the man as Michael Mort and laughed with embarrassed relief. "Oh my God! You scared me!"

Michael stood, half shrouded in darkness, the light from the street lamps dancing across his face in strange patterns with the movement of the leaves in the trees. From where Sarah was standing, it looked like he was changing rapidly, his image flickering and throbbing as if captured on old celluloid film. He looked older than seventeen in that light. Much older. His jaw was sharp and angular, punctuated at the chin with a coal-black goatee. His lips were full and curved, his black hair streaming over his shoulders and down the back of his trench coat. He was beautiful, she thought— almost too beautiful. The kind of dark and brooding good looks that earned him sideways glances from girls harbouring secret lust, too timid to risk his thinly veiled disdain. He was different, and wanted to make sure that everyone was aware of it with his aloof and disaffected manner. Sarah felt the pull of attraction, despite her better judgment. He could be the devil for all she knew. What had Donna said, about him stalking her? She held John's guitar a little tighter.

"What are you doing back here?" she demanded.

"Just hanging out," he said. He shifted his knapsack on his shoulder. The knapsack was covered in pins, with names of older bands that Sarah had only heard of from John. Black

Flag, Flipper, Reagan Youth, 7Seconds, Minor Threat, Dag Nasty, The Exploited, Hüsker Dü. There was something dangling from his fingers, too. It was the leaf.

"I was looking for that," she said.

Michael held the leaf up, inspecting it indifferently before offering it to her. "Take it," he said, stepping from the shadows.

Their fingers touched briefly as a gust of wind plucked the leaf from Michael's fingers and carried it up into the night.

"Oh!" Sarah cried. She quickly collected herself and regarded him with mild chagrin. "I collect leaves," she shyly confessed. "Pretty dumb, huh?"

Michael looked back at her, unflinching. He didn't shift his eyes or look at his feet when he talked to her like so many other guys she knew. It made her nervous and excited just to stand next to him.

"I collect comics," he said, his tone friendlier. "How dumb is that?"

They laughed with the surprise of spontaneous fellowship and she noticed for the first time that his irises were completely black. They stared at each other, the laughter trickling away, until only their smiles were left. Her heart fluttered in her chest like a bird scrambling inside a box and she found herself wondering what it would be like to press her mouth against his lips, to taste him. As she considered this, a voice called her name from across the street.

It was Peter. He jogged over to where they stood, glanced at Michael, then turned his back to him, addressing Sarah as though Michael weren't there. "You walking home?"

Sarah opened her mouth to answer, but said nothing. She didn't want to go off with Peter and spend the next half hour dodging his advances. She wanted to stay in the half-formed light beside the library and learn more about Michael. "I'm okay, Peter," she said.

"I don't mind walking you home. I go that way anyway. You know that."

Sarah looked over at Michael. He had a bemused smirk on his face, waiting for her answer. Peter waited too.

"I'm okay, Peter, really. I've got some stuff to do."

Peter nodded. "Yeah, sure." He glared at Michael as he turned to leave, took a few steps, then turned around again. "Don't forget the party at my place. You don't want to miss it." He pointed his finger at Sarah like a pistol and cocked his thumb.

Sarah winced inside. She hated when he did that. "Sure, great. Thanks." She watched him go, willed him to leave faster, the sound of his green Keds growing fainter as they squeaked against the wet pavement in the distance. Michael was watching her. "Don't ask," she said.

He held his hands innocently in the air. "Hey, it's none of my business who you go out with."

"Oh, God, please." Sarah rolled her eyes. "He won't leave me alone."

"Like moths to a flame," Michael said.

Was he making fun of her? She looked at him, expecting him to make a joke of it. But he wasn't laughing. He was just staring intently back at her with his dark eyes. She tried to grasp something clever to say but came up empty-handed. Now she was the one examining her feet.

"What I really want to know," he said, rescuing her from her awkwardness, "is what kind of music you play on that guitar."

Relieved to change the subject, Sarah dismissed her interest with a laugh, talking rapidly. "It's my brother's guitar—John. He was amazing. I'm not very good. I just fool around a bit because I can't stand the idea of his guitar just sitting around not being played." She stopped, wondering if she should explain. She never talked about this stuff with anyone. Sadness made people uncomfortable, she discovered, especially if it went on too long. She felt suddenly naked, balancing on a very steep cliff, toes stuck dangerously over the edge. It would be so easy to just tell him, to free herself from the burden of it. Holding her breath for a moment, she spoke the word at last. "Cancer." It tumbled out as she surrendered to the moment, relinquishing control. It felt so good to let go.

Michael nodded. He didn't take his eyes from her, or fidget, the way other people did when she talked like this. He didn't try to comfort her with words, or some story about a relative who had died in a similar way. Instead, he looked back at her, with simple honesty and genuine emotion. She felt the band begin to loosen around her heart, the air rushing into her lungs as though for the first time. Should she tell him about John's ghost, too? Was it too soon for that kind of intimacy?

"Do you want to see his guitar?" she asked.

He held the guitar with reverence, admiring the finish. "A Fender Strat. It's beautiful."

Sarah couldn't help beaming. "You know it?"

"Know it? It's vintage. This is a piece of history." Michael strummed the strings lightly, fingering a few chords before handing it back to her. "I can't wait to hear you play."

"You'll have to wait a while," she said, placing the guitar gently in its case. "I just started. I'm pretty brutal. I'm better at collecting leaves," she added, smiling.

"Hey, let me walk you home," he offered brightly, as if it

were an original idea. "I don't want your old man to get worried."

Sarah snapped the guitar case shut. Her "old man." She'd tell Michael about him some other time.

CHAPTER TWO

Sarah lay in bed, the covers pulled up to her chin. There'd been a noise outside her bedroom door. A soft sound, like a sigh. Too terrified to move, she listened intently and waited, expecting John to appear beside the bed again. She wanted to turn on the light but was afraid to expose her hand from beneath the safety of the blankets, so she just lay there, begging him silently to stay away, choosing her thoughts carefully so as not to incur his wrath. Who knew what ghosts were capable of? She had no doubt that he could read her mind. Anything that could come back from the dead had to be able to do that. She tried to control her breathing but it was noisy and quick. Loud enough to wake the dead. *No, no, don't think that.*

She glanced at the bottle of aspirin on the milk crate beside her bed. As if on cue, the faint pulse of a headache began to work its way up the back of her neck. Her eyes flickered around the room. If she reached her hand out for the aspirin bottle, would he grab it? She couldn't take that chance. Her thoughts hopscotched from childhood images of John to demonic ghosts circling her bed. Forcing good thoughts to the forefront, she attempted to subdue her fear, to trick the ghost into thinking that she wasn't afraid. Her temples throbbed as the pain crept up to its usual spot across her brow. She squeezed her eyes shut and quickly opened them again, then shot her hand out and plucked the aspirin bottle from the crate. Snapping her hand back under the covers, she waited. Nothing happened. She was okay.

Sarah clicked on the light, swallowed a couple aspirins, then got up and walked over to her dresser. From the bottom drawer she produced an old shoebox and two red plastic binders marked "Photos." Sitting with one foot tucked beneath her on the bed, she began flipping through one of the binders. She always looked at them in the same order. Chronologically. Except for the photos she kept in the box, the ones of the family before she came along. She kept them separate, because there was something about them that seemed to warrant it. Her father was in all of those early pictures—handsome, several years older than her mother. Holding John as an infant, as a toddler, playing ball with his son. The house neater, well appointed, her mother's near-frantic expressions of joy. All of this seemed to change when Sarah was born, seven years after John. The atmosphere in the house cooling, a shabbiness settling like frost over everything, her father's slow migration out of the camera's view.

Turning the page, Sarah stopped to study a Christmas photo. It showed her and John beaming in front of the tree, the doll she had received that year slumped in a small wooden chair off to one side. John wearing a cowboy outfit, the holster slung low over his hips, hat tilted back. In the background, her mother sat with one arm draped across her knees, hair covered in the requisite kerchief, skin as pale as the soles of her new terrycloth slippers, her gaze trained on some vanishing point in the distance. And then her father, outside the frame for the most part, only his legs visible from his favourite chair, the accompanying black glass ash-tray on its brass stand, the ever-present tumbler of scotch clasped in one hand, poised. The alcohol that had infused every part of their life, tolerated by her mother like an embarrassing relative. Had he ever loved any of them? Always justifying his road warrior lifestyle with some delusion of "hitting it big," of "landing the big fish," the perfect opportunity just waiting to be capitalized on, the promise of better things to come. His sudden rushes of exuberance, the attempts at affection, her mother's refusal, pushing him away in the kitchen: *Leave me alone!* And Sarah's guilty voyeurism, watching through the kitchen window from her spot among the bergamot. Why wouldn't she give daddy another chance? But, *no, no, no, eighteen miserable years for what?* And later his dedication to the job turned out to be a front, a pantomime, masking his true desire to be free. Her mother's silent hatred filling the house, the dishes clattering out accusations in the sink. *Craven.*

John was the brave one, with his attempted escape from the joyless carousel of family life until the illness pulled him back in. Sarah felt the familiar ache resonating in her chest, the warm buzz reaching her cheeks as the clouds of grief gathered. Would the hole in her heart ever heal? She had filled it with anything she could find—the cold fist of anger, the liquid drip of sorrow, the anesthetizing patch of drugs and alcohol—but still the hole whistled and gaped, refusing to mend. Tears blurred her vision as she looked at the photos. Their Christmases were more obligations than celebrations, a vestigial ritual upheld by weary parents. It had been worse at the hospital, though.

Most of the patients on the west wing's third floor hadn't a clue that it was Christmas. The rest made shrines of the few cards they received, the occasional installation punctuated by a blood-red poinsettia, which the nurses often confiscated. In the sterile and controlled world of chronic care, a poinsettia was a potentially lethal object, believed to harbour enough poison to kill a curious forager. Visiting hours would not be extended despite the season and the two-visitor rule would not be bent. This was not a concern for most of the visitors.

Christmas was a difficult time for chronic care staff, who silently begrudged the care of patients that offered no hope of healing, Christmas miracles aside. It was much merrier in the obstetrics ward with the bundles of new babies to help ring in the holidays. More than one nurse entered Room 319 smelling mysteriously of alcohol, officious voices grating to a higher than normal pitch.

New Year's Eve was even harder to bear. A covert visit had to be arranged. Sneaking by the nurses' station, past the gaping doorways that lined the hall, "Happy New Year" whispered through the dark, voices hushed so as not to be heard, until the nurse appeared, glaring, in the doorway.

Sarah snapped the binder shut and gathered up the photos, returning them to the bottom drawer. She wouldn't think about sad things right now. She wouldn't think about ghosts or anything else that frightened her either. She would think about Michael. Slipping back beneath the covers, she stared across the room and waited for sleep to come.

* * *

Donna jumped on her as soon as she entered the classroom. "Where were you last night?" She pursed her lips and popped her gum accusingly, narrowing her black-ringed eyes as she rested her oxblood Doc Martens on top of Sarah's desk.

Sarah shoved Donna's feet to the floor. "Do you mind?"

"I know where you were."

"Is that right?" Sarah dug through her knapsack, checking to see if she'd brought the right books to class. "And how do you know that, super sleuth?"

"Peter told me."

"Peter?" Sarah feigned composure. That weasel. Of course he'd told her.

"Yeah. He said you and Mortimer were right chummy with each other."

"Stop calling him that."

"So Peter was right, then?"

There was no hiding now. "Yeah, Peter was right. Michael walked me home, that's all. What's wrong with that?"

"Michael, huh? So now you're on a first-name basis? That's how it starts. Did he try to touch you?"

"Who's the pervert here, Donna?" Sarah snapped. "Get your kicks somewhere else. God, sometimes you're so weird."

"I can see you're still feeling *sensitive*."

"That's right." Sarah stood up, flung her bag onto her shoulder and marched from the room. She wasn't swallowing any of Donna's poison today. The last thing she needed was to be interrogated. Donna was such an idiot sometimes, the way she pushed things. She was a wildcard, a loose cannon, always getting Sarah in trouble, or embarrassing her, or getting her kicked out of places she didn't want to get kicked out of. She was a liability with her aggressive ways, always going on about something—or nothing. At least it seemed like nothing to Sarah.

The sunlight was blinding as she burst into the alleyway, escaping the sombre atmosphere of the school and the hordes of students crowding to get in. The day was bright and cool. A perfect fall day. A perfect day to skip class. A group of stoners stood smoking in a huddle against the wall. Sarah wondered what it would be like to be stoned that early in the morning. Some kids did it all the time. One guy had even passed out in class once. The school had instated locker inspections immediately after. *Good work*, Sarah thought as she walked past the group, a cloud of smoke hanging over them like a prophecy. One guy waved her over, offering a toke. She shook her head and smiled politely, continued to walk down the alley before dipping through the bushes to the street. She didn't know where she should go. The Queen's, maybe. If it was open. She'd never gone there so early before. Walking briskly, she avoided the eyes of adults, afraid they would wonder why she wasn't in school. Busybodies.

When she reached the Queen's, Sarah looked through the window into the diner. The row of faded green stools stood empty before the melamine counter, the soda fountains dulled from years of fryer grease and use since the fifties. Wooden booths hugged the wall, individual jukeboxes poised at every table. The black-and-white floor tiles were scuffed in a trail down the middle of the shop past the booths toward the washrooms. The whole place was like a postcard from the past, including the owner who slouched over the counter reading the paper, his swollen belly permanently diapered in a stained white apron. Nick the Prick. He hated students, even though they gave him most of his business. Sarah wondered briefly what he would look like naked, his soft white skin jiggling like milk-coloured Jello. *Yuck,* she thought as she pushed against the door.

The bell jangled loudly in the morning quiet. Nick didn't bother to look up from his paper. Taking her usual seat in a booth near the back, Sarah pulled her writing journal and a pen from her knapsack. Nick finally acknowledged her, waddling over, face carved with disdain. He sloshed a glass of water onto the table.

"What do you want?"

"Coffee," Sarah said. "And, uh . . . fries."

Nick shook his head. "Too early for fries."

"Okay . . . toast," Sarah said, ". . . with jam."

Nick sauntered to the kitchen and disappeared through the swinging doors. Sarah clicked her pen and began to write. She started writing about Donna, about how mad she was. She would write her anger away, put it down on paper so she could forget about it. Defuse it. That's what she did with everything. Her feelings about her father and her mother, her yawning emptiness over John. Her terror at seeing him . . . it . . . again. She couldn't actually bring herself to write the word "ghost." To put it down in ink would make it seem too real. But she *would* write it, she told herself, the same way she had scratched out her entire existence over the years in short spiky letters. The highs and lows of it. The little peaks and valleys of an imperfect life.

After writing several lines about Donna, Sarah found herself thinking about Michael. In fact, she couldn't *stop* thinking about him. The leisurely walk home, the talk of music and books. The conversation had been easy, with genuine interest on both sides. He had asked lots of questions about her. He seemed to really care. It made her feel surprisingly dizzy and light just to think about him, like the way she felt when she jumped from the cliff at the quarry. The momentary weightlessness as her body lifted up, then descended. The whistle of wind in her ears. The sparkling sheet of blue, rushing up to meet her. She floated there when she thought of him, just above the point of impact. A kind of crystalline suspension. Until she was struck by the horrifying realization that she hadn't asked a single question about him. How could she have been so stupid? The water rose up as her body hit the surface with a slap, her heart sinking like a stone.

The pain swelled in her head again, sending Sarah digging through her bag for the bottle of aspirin. She found it just as Nick appeared shambling over with the coffee and toast. No jam. Sarah sighed, poked at the flaccid white bread soaked in margarine and pushed the plate to one side. She didn't feel like toast anyway. The coffee smelled particularly bitter today, too. She diluted it with cream, carefully peeling the aluminum tabs off the creamers and neatly stacking the empty containers next to the abandoned toast. Normally she didn't take sugar, but this morning she felt she needed it, pouring it straight from the dispenser into her cup. Two more creamers were added and another dose of sugar for good measure. When the coffee met with her approval, Sarah opened the aspirin bottle and rattled four into her hand, checked the dosage on the label and returned one. A quick gulp of water washed the pills down. Reaching for her coffee, Sarah sipped it slowly and considered what she would do with the rest of her day. She wouldn't allow herself to be spooked, she promised herself that. But it was easy to be brave in the daylight. *Just keep thinking about Michael,* she told herself.

That's what you should do. Her mind drifted over his features and came to rest on Donna's query: "Did he try to touch you?"

No, Donna, he didn't. Didn't try to touch her. Didn't try to kiss her or even hold her hand, but walked patiently beside her up the sidewalk to her door, waiting calmly at the bottom of the stairs until the key turned in the lock. A smile and a wave. She had waited for something more, her hips pressed against the railing, leaning toward him, her long brown hair tumbling down like a confession. He hadn't tried anything. Maybe he wasn't attracted to her in that way? She couldn't accept this. She knew the effect she had on men.

Even the doctors at the hospital seemed somehow drawn to her. The questioning look in their eyes. The way they said hello. Like they'd been waiting to see her. Counting the minutes of their day to the time when she'd be in it. She had accommodated them in the beginning by taking care of herself, making sure she was presentable when they were due to arrive. It gave her a thrill at first to think about them thinking about her. Until later on, when things got bad and she found she just didn't care about anything any more, especially the desire of doctors.

The bell on the restaurant door jingled abruptly and some students bustled in. Must be on spare, Sarah thought. Lifting the cup to her mouth, she rested the rim against her bottom lip, breathing in the warmth of the coffee without drinking. She let her eyes relax, the words of her journal blurring like ink in the rain. She thought about seeing Michael again, thought about how she would arrange it. Sipping the coffee

26

at last, she let the warm liquid pool at the back of her throat before swallowing. She would see him soon, she decided; she would see him tonight.

＊　＊　＊

Sarah moved along the street, past the bakery and the shops full of "old-people" clothes. Past the city hall and the police station, ducking through alleys where she could to avoid attention. She followed the street to the south end, with its squat bungalows that all looked the same. Dirty windows, aluminum siding, tarpaper, chipboard, asphalt shingles, forgotten dogs on short chains, neglected children with snotty noses and messy hair. The low part of town. That's what her mother called it. Sarah walked by all of it toward the old stone bridge that arched over the railway tracks to the train station. At one time her mother would have been furious if she'd known Sarah was there. But she didn't know. And she would never know about it, or the place Sarah called her "secret spot."

Her sneakers slipped over the gravel as she navigated down the hill to the right of the bridge, one hand skimming along the ground for balance. At the bottom, Sarah skidded to a stop. Stepping gingerly onto the train tracks, she advanced like a tightrope artist, arms held out at her sides, toes dipping dramatically, one after the other, as she moved along the rail. When she reached the abandoned boxcar she jumped to the ground. The car was covered in tags and graffiti, the worn letters of *Norfolk Southern* faded to a broken outline.

Checking up and down the tracks to make sure she was alone, Sarah pulled herself into the boxcar. It seemed as black as a cave after the glare of the sun. The smell of piss and stale beer caught in the back of her throat as she waited for her eyes to adjust, then glanced quickly around. No ghosts. The floor was littered with the usual trash: bits of crumpled newspaper, discarded bottles, cigarette butts.

It was dangerous to hang out at the tracks, she knew that. There was that girl, last summer, raped beneath the bridge. Someone from one of the other high schools. Alone, after dark. Sarah never went to her secret spot at night after hearing that. The boxcar was close enough to the station to be safe during the day when the workers were about. Yet there was still a certain thrill in being there, even in the daylight. It was quiet. It was quiet at the cemetery, too. She liked to hang out there as well. Not for bad reasons. To look at the flowers and read the headstones. Sometimes she would gather pieces of tombstones that had been knocked apart by vandals and try to return them to their rightful places. She felt oddly close to people there. It was peaceful.

A bundle of old papers functioned as a makeshift cushion in one corner of the car. Sarah sat down. The boxcar seemed lonelier than usual in the filtered light. She couldn't help wondering if John's ghost could find her there, if it would stalk her like a poltergeist. There were movies about things like that—ghosts following people everywhere, moving from town to town. She loved John, though. Would he really hurt her? Her mind skipped over the surface of reason like a pebble. Maybe ghosts were devoid of emotion, she thought. Or maybe they haunted people because they couldn't help it, because they were drawn to life the same way a vampire is drawn to blood. Because vampires, even when they love someone, have to fight the urge to feed on human flesh. But it was no good to think like that. She was just freaking herself out.

A cigarette was what she needed. It would help her to relax. Leaning against the wall of the boxcar, she opened her purse and searched around for her lighter and cigarettes. Marlboros. John had gotten her hooked on the brand when she was fifteen. He used to sneak her cartons that he bought at the duty-free whenever he would cross the border. Hiding out in the shed, he showed her the proper way to smoke so she wouldn't do it "like a girl." Now it was part of her, a habit she couldn't break, out of deference to him. It was their ritual, and they had found ways to get away with it as long as they could.

It was more of an excuse just to get outside at first, huddling on the small patch of grass behind the hospital, the occasional shared experience with some other prisoner who had managed to escape the nurses' tyranny. Then it became an imperative, the only bit of familiar in an otherwise foreign world. Until the craving for nicotine was subsumed by sheer exhaustion and finally, the absence of desire altogether.

Sarah straightened the crumpled packet. Would Michael approve of her habit? She thought about Donna, calling him Mortimer. That made her laugh, in spite of herself, and she suddenly wished that Donna were with her, playing hooky in the boxcar. Donna would chase the ghosts away. She would make jokes about it and play it down so that Sarah could just let the whole thing go. She decided that she would tell Donna about John, the first chance she got.

A sharp tap on the pack of Marlboros produced a cigarette. Sarah shook her disposable lighter, then struck the flint wheel with her thumb. The flint sparked several times before the flame finally shot up, flickering blue and orange in the diffuse light. Mesmerized by its hypnotic dance, she imagined herself inside the flame, the chaos of molecules colliding, the fire folding and unfolding, consuming the bone. It lapped greedily at the end of the cigarette as she drew quick puffs, the tobacco glowing a brilliant orange by the time she released her thumb from the flint. Taking a long drag, she held the smoke in, then slowly released it, the smoke rising over her top lip and up into her nostrils the way John had taught her, like a fugitive spirit escaped and devoured.

The nicotine worked its way swiftly through her veins, delivering its calm. Sarah reached into the small pocket at the front of her knapsack and pulled out a neat bundle of photos. These were her favourite ones, the ones she kept with her always. A silver paper clip and a slip of folded newsprint protected them. She unwrapped the bundle. A ten-year-old John laughed back at her, the photo slightly blurry and yellowed around the edges. But there was no mistaking her brother's smile. Her three-year-old self beamed up at him standing in the middle of a blue plastic wading pool in a pink bikini, tummy bulging out. John, shirtless in cut-off jean shorts, his hard little body all bones and sinew. Her mother and father lounging in aluminum deck chairs on the grass behind the pool. And always the mystery girl standing in the background. Who was she? An aunt, an older girl from the neighbourhood? Sarah refused to ask her mother about it. That would have meant they'd actually have to talk to each other. She would rather figure it out herself; it was her little mystery.

In every picture, the girl's face was obscured by sunlight, the details erased in the glare, her features always blurred, hidden. There was something familiar about her, though, something she couldn't quite put her finger on. The smile? The clothes? The way the light seemed to radiate from her and no one else?

When she was finished with the photos, Sarah carefully placed them in order before wrapping them back in the paper. Securing them with the paper clip, she returned them to the pocket of her knapsack, then stopped to massage her temples lightly. The aspirin hadn't worked. She would have to take more. She inspected her cigarette. Nearly finished. Tapping another from the pack, she lit it off the butt of the first, then extinguished the spent cigarette on the floor of the boxcar, flicking it adeptly against the wall away from the newspapers. She practised blowing smoke rings, the undulating white hoops suspended like questions in the still air, expanding, curling, dissipating. She thought of Michael sitting in class. Was he thinking about her? Her face flushed at the thought of it and she wondered at the depth of her emotions for him. It was quite fascinating, really, how she was drawn to him in a way that she couldn't understand or explain, as though every atom in her body longed for union with his. It had been like that from the very first, when she'd seen him standing outside the school. She couldn't convey this to anyone—especially Donna, who had taken an instant dislike to him, as if Sarah's interest in Michael were somehow a threat to their friendship.

Sarah envisioned Michael leaving class, imagined him

walking along the street, past the library toward home. That was how she would do it. She would wait behind the library, then follow him. When it was safe, when no one else would see, she would catch up to him. She drew the smoke deep into her lungs and exhaled, the smoke billowing in a satisfying plume in the air.

CHAPTER THREE

E xcept for a few students loitering in the alley, the
schoolyard was empty. Sarah leaned against the
library wall, hidden in the afternoon shadows.
From where she was standing, she could see two sets of
doors. There was a strange electricity in the air. The maple
trees quivered with the weight of it, anticipating the bell,
the ring splitting the silence at last. The doors to the school
flung open and a stream of students poured out. Girls in
low-cut jeans, hoop earrings, their long hair flowing, the
sex of them available like supermarket oranges. Boys in
baseball caps and skater pants, wrestling, laughing, jockey-
ing for supremacy. Donna appeared at the far doors. Stopping to light a cigarette, she forced the other students to
course around her. She took her time, adjusted her jacket,
blew smoke like a signal into the fall air. Sarah couldn't
help laughing. At least Donna didn't disappoint.

When she had made her point, Donna finally walked
down the stairs and into the alley, taking the shortcut to the
main street. Going to the Queen's for a cup of j, no doubt.
Biding her time until something of interest came along. She

slipped behind the school and was gone. That's when Sarah noticed Michael. He was already a block from the school walking past the library on the other side of the street. How had she missed him? His long hair was pulled back in a ponytail, knapsack slung casually over one shoulder. He wore an ankle-length khaki trench coat, combat boots, black pants. Controlled anger.

The bird scrambled frantically in her chest. She waited, counting beats until Michael was several blocks down the street, then stepped out of the shadows to follow.

Michael walked toward the tracks. Sarah held back, careful not to get too close, even though she was uncertain about what it was that she was afraid of. Being seen with Michael? Running into someone she knew? The wind picked up, the trees quaking in response, shaking their colourful leaves like medicine rattles. Michael responded in kind, releasing the tie holding his hair, his raven mane flowing in the breeze. How magical he looked—and wild, Sarah thought. As marvellous and mythical against the backdrop of derelict south-side houses as a winged horse. People watched as he walked by. Not boldly, but circumspectly, and with great interest. He seemed aloof to their attention, like a king, walking as if the world were laid out for his purpose alone. This made Sarah even more intent on knowing him, on getting closer.

Watching him walk over the bridge, she jumped behind a row of bushes when he glanced in her direction, then waited until he reached the other side of the tracks before crossing the bridge herself. As soon as he reached the park, Michael dematerialized behind a stand of pine trees.

Sarah trotted along the sidewalk, waiting for several breaths behind the trees, then moving into the park. Scanning the stretch of green, she could see the boathouse perched on the edge of the pond near a small concrete dam. There was a low, red-brick building that housed the public washrooms, always closed or under surveillance, and rows of empty cages that had once held peacocks and other exotic birds. In every direction, hydro wires sliced across the sky, crisscrossing and knitting together at several giant towers beside the dam. A ten-foot-high chain-link fence stood sentry around the towers, the regulation red lightning bolt sign threatening trespassers with immediate electrocution. Behind the towers stood the faded tents and food stands of an uninspired and weary fair, the rides frozen against a backdrop of grey. But Michael was nowhere to be seen. Sarah stood searching the horizon when a voice broke the silence.

"Why are you following me?"

It was Michael, staring at her from among the pine trees. She flushed with embarrassment, having been caught. "I wasn't spying on you or anything."

He looked at her skeptically.

"I—I just wanted to know where you live," she confessed.

"Why didn't you just ask me?"

Why *hadn't* she just asked him? She wasn't even sure herself. "You're right. I'm sorry. I guess I was being nosy," she said, trying to recover her cool.

He didn't answer, but came out from the trees and began walking across the park. Sarah padded after him. They walked in silence, she too flustered to attempt conversation, and then strangely, profoundly enervated. *It's the power lines,* she thought, *draining my energy.*

"Your dad's a prof?" she ventured, a tone of apology in her voice.

"Is that what your friend told you?"

"Who, Donna?"

He stopped short, aware of her deceit.

"Um, yeah, Donna said so, about your dad, I mean," she stammered.

"She's a real ace, isn't she?" he said. "A real private eye."

She couldn't believe Donna was getting her in trouble again. Her fidelity to her friend quickly vanished. She wanted to blame her for everything, then felt immediately ashamed of herself for that. "Why do you stare at me in class?" she impulsively demanded, reversing the attack.

Michael turned and began walking again. Sarah was pleased with her clever tactic, although his *sang-froid* unnerved her still; it made her feel somehow inadequate. They cut across the parking lot and began climbing the hill to the north end of the park, the grass fringed brown from an early frost, the hill bisected by a thin dirt path that zig-zagged like a scar through its middle.

"Kids toboggan here in the winter," she said.

He frowned, refusing to throw her a line.

"I still come sometimes," she continued to chatter. For some reason she couldn't stop herself now. *It's the power lines*, she thought again, *controlling my mind*. "What do you like to do? When you're not in school, I mean."

"Well, I don't spend all day whacking off, despite what your friend thinks."

Sarah laughed. It was funny to hear him say it. "She's a jerk," she said. "She's full of it. I wouldn't take anything she says to heart."

"Oh, I don't," he said coolly. "It's you I'm worried about."

"Me?" Sarah exclaimed, stopping in her tracks. "Why are you worried about me?"

He faced her, the hint of a sneer on his lips. "You seem . . . easily influenced."

"What? I am not." But she couldn't prevent the colour from rising in her cheeks. It was as good as an admission. "Donna doesn't influence me," she said, her voice betraying her.

He shrugged. "Okay, fine. What do I care?"

This was too much, Sarah thought. Of course he cared. Wasn't that why he stared at her all the time in class? Wasn't that why she was here, on this frost-scorched hill, following this path? She felt suddenly stupid and insignificant. "Well, is he or isn't he?" she pressed.

"As a matter of fact, he's a doctor. Palliative care. Harvard Medical School for those who are easily impressed."

"So what are you doing here, in Terrace?" she asked, ignoring his sarcasm.

He let out a sigh. "Convenience. Compromise."

She waited for an explanation, but he didn't offer one.

"I don't get it."

"Between my mom and dad. Except they forgot to ask me if I care. And I do. I'd rather not be here. But I'll be free of it all soon enough."

Free of it. Sarah wondered what that would feel like, to be so sure of something. She'd never even considered the idea of leaving her mother behind now that John was gone. Somewhere in her mind a small window opened, the breeze of possibility floating in. "How do you get on with your dad?"

Michael looked at her warily. "You're a regular private eye too." But then his voice softened. "My old man's all right. We have an understanding."

Sarah nodded. It sounded healthy. She felt him let his guard down, loosen, like a fist unclenching. He had every right to be defensive, she thought. She *had* been following him. *Who's the stalker now, Donna?*

They came to the top of the hill in front of an olive-coloured board-and-batten cottage, solid, although faded, like the tents of the small fair. It nested beneath a stand of old spruce trees that leaned protectively over it.

"Is this it?"

"Yeah. Want to come in?" He didn't wait for her answer but moved around to the back of the house. Sarah followed and watched as he produced a key flashing like a goldfish on the end of a string and used it to jimmy the frame on the window. Pushing the window open with the ease of familiar repetition, he tossed his bag through and slipped into the house, as agile as a cat. "Throw your bag in," he called out.

Sarah hoisted her bag through the window.

"Use the rock by your feet to get a foot up."

Sarah stepped on the rock and laughed. "What's wrong with using the door?" she asked.

He grabbed her hands and pulled her shrieking and laughing through the window, letting her fall onto the bed below, a tangle of hair and clothes. The secret of his private life was suddenly revealed through posters, books, comics, belongings.

Sarah looked at him beside her on the bed. "Well," she said, "you have a B & E career ahead of you if you decide not to finish school." Then she added, "Have you always been this neat?"

He stood and removed his jacket, a hint of tattoo showing beneath his shirtsleeve. Sarah couldn't help noticing it—and the rest of his body. His waist was firm, his arms sculpted and strong. She was happy she had decided to wear her tight blue blouse and her good bra. She pointed at a box on the shelf across the room. "You play Monopoly," she said, trying to sound nonchalant. "Which piece are you?"

"Thimble."

"No way!" Her laughter filled the room. "Nobody's the thimble! I took you for a cannon or a dog . . . a boot, maybe . . ."

"What about you?"

"Oh, I'm a dog, for sure."

He smiled knowingly. "I wouldn't say that."

Sarah smiled too, until she remembered John's ghost standing beside her bed. But she didn't want to think of her brother that way. She wouldn't allow it. She wanted to remember him the way he used to be. "My brother was the cannon—appropriately enough, seeing as he always blew me out of the water. I don't know why I bothered playing at all, he always beat me. I can't believe you're the thimble."

"Believe it. What do you want to drink?" he asked, taking her coat and knapsack and tossing them onto a worn yellow upholstered chair in the corner of the room. Her bundle of photos dropped onto the floor. He retrieved the package, examining it. "What's this?"

Sarah jumped up and grabbed the bundle from his hand. "Just some photos. You wouldn't be interested."

"How do you know?"

"They're just boring photos."

"So boring you carry them around in that anal little bundle?"

"Yeah, kind of." Sarah stuffed the photos back into her knapsack, zipping the pocket shut.

"You've got a secret," he said.

She brushed the hair from her eyes defiantly. "Doesn't everyone?"

Michael leaned against the doorframe, folding his arms across his chest. "What would you like to drink?" he asked again.

"Just a soda if you have one."

Sarah took the opportunity to peruse his room. The neat shelves, the rows of cyberpunk and sci-fi books, CDs, movie action figures, old VHS tapes labelled and dated, a small TV, VCR beneath it, magazine organizers full of comics stored in neat plastic bags. Beside the single bed a small wooden desk supporting a PC clone with a nineteen-inch screen—and not a speck of dust anywhere. Running one finger along the shelf, she inspected it for dirt.

"Who's your favourite?" she called out. She could hear the sound of ice clinking into glasses, the fridge door thumping closed. Michael appeared with two blue tumblers filled with cola, the soda sizzling and foaming against the ice. He handed her a glass, then took a sip from the other.

"Thanks." Sarah took a quick gulp and felt the burn of carbonation and rum across her tongue. She choked, caught her breath. "Isn't it a little early to be drinking?"

He laughed and tilted his drink back, draining half the glass.

Sarah pointed at the rows of comics. "Who's your favourite?"

"Favourite what?"

"Comic guy."

"Superhero or character? There's a difference."

"I don't know . . . superhero. Who's your favourite one?"

He pulled a magazine organizer from the shelf and removed a comic, handing it to her. "Dark Knight–era

Batman. Definitely the top of my superhero list. But I love anything Frank Miller does," he added, as if she would know what he was talking about. Taking another organizer from the shelf, he searched through the comics. "My favourite comic book *character* has to be Judge Dredd, the U. K. version, in *2000 A.D.*, by Garth Ennis and Steve Dillon." He selected a comic and handed it to her like a rare vase. "They cross over."

"What do you mean?" Sarah asked, glancing casually at the comics.

"The characters. They cross over. Sometimes they're featured together. Dark Knight Batman and Judge Dredd are like two opposing aspects of the law. Judge Dredd, he's the letter of the law. But Batman, he represents justice."

Sarah nodded dumbly, completely taken aback by his knowledge and the depth of his interest. She politely examined the dark graphics on the covers more closely. They reminded her of an old photo of John, holding one of his favourite comics, the picture taken just before he decided to embark on his great adventure at the age of twelve. He'd planned it for months, inspired by an ad in the back of an old DC Superman comic, next to the sea monkeys and "X-ray spex" and the Charles Atlas strip promising to turn any ninety-seven-pound weakling into a hulking he-man. *"Giant submarine! Incredible detail!"*

"You can be the co-pilot," he had told her so that she would help him. And she did, stealing the money from the back of the toilet where her father had left his change. When the package finally arrived it contained a cardboard submarine folded to fit the brown manila envelope. She would never forget his look of confusion and disgust, or the sound of her father's scathing laughter, his raucous rendition of the Beatles' "Yellow Submarine" booming through the house. It was she who rescued the loathsome submarine from the trash and kept it for years, until it was eventually destroyed when the basement flooded.

"John loved Superman," she said.

"Your brother?"

"Yeah, he loved Superman. Batman too, but Superman was his all-time favourite. He told me once that Batman was going to come and beat Superman up, and then a new era would start. I think he was really sad about it." She grinned sheepishly at how ridiculous the whole thing sounded.

"You gotta love Superman," Michael said. "He's a class act." He gestured to the comics in her hands. "You can take them out of the plastic if you want. I just keep them like that so they don't get wrecked."

"It's okay," she said, handing him back the comics. "I bet you're the only one who's ever touched these copies."

He laughed at her insight.

Continuing to inspect the shelves, Sarah stopped when she reached the action figures. She picked one up. "Who's the messed-up guy with the chainsaw?"

"Ash, from Evil Dead 2. A personal favourite."

"Pretty hardcore."

"You know it. He cuts off his own hand when evil possesses it and straps this chainsaw to his arm so he can fight the undead."

Sarah looked at him in wonder. "You're really into this stuff, huh?"

"Yeah. It's my *thang*." He took the figure from her and replaced it precisely on the shelf.

"Your music . . ." Sarah started to ask. "You're into retro . . .

alternative . . . ?" She groped for a label. The rum was taking effect, warming her with the earthy kick of fermented molasses, the sweet cola over top.

"Some. But Mike Patton—he's a genius. I've got all his work."

Sarah touched the rim of her glass seductively with her tongue. "Play something for me. Play the one you like the most."

Searching the row of CDs, Michael selected one from the stack. He held it up for her to see. "Fantomas, *Amenaza Al Mundo*." He loaded it in the player and adjusted the sound. The music rose, filling the room. It flooded the empty space between them, sealing the fissures of uncertainty. They listened in silence, Michael watching her face for her reaction.

"Anna Kournikova," Sarah impetuously announced over the music.

"What about her?"

"I want someone to name a virus after me like Anna Kournikova. Then I'd be famous."

He leaned toward her, took the glass from her hand. "Is that what you want . . . to be famous?"

"Yes, I do," she said, tossing her hair back.

He moved closer still, leaning in, their breath mingling, the smell of rum and sugar intoxicating. "Did you know that some natives believe you steal a little piece of their soul every time you take their picture?"

Sarah felt the heat of his body. "Donna calls you Mortimer," she said.

"That's creative."

Touching the edge of his sleeve, she pushed it up, revealing his skin, the colour of coffee and cream. "I want to see it."

He stood, rolled the fabric to his shoulder. The shock of green ink on tawny skin. Sarah outlined the design lightly with her finger. "What is it? A werewolf?"

"Coyote. Trickster. Creator. Shape-shifter. He stole fire from the ancients to keep the human race warm."

Sarah pointed to an elongated horizontal figure eight floating above the coyote's head like a halo. "What's this?"

"Lemniscate."

Sarah knit her brow in confusion.

"The symbol for infinity."

"Ahhh," she said knowingly, even though she wasn't quite sure of its significance. At once she was aware that he was out of her league, that he knew things—important things. She felt somehow lazy and wanting, like she had spent all her time smoking cigarettes and drinking coffee while he had been exploring the world. "I thought Prometheus stole fire," she said, challenging him.

He regarded her with amusement. "That's one mythology. But native Indians credit Coyote."

"Why is he standing on two legs like that?"

"Because Coyote can assume human form."

The wires finally connected in her head. "You're native?"

"I'm half," he said with some pride. "At least, that's what I was told."

"What do you mean? Don't your parents know?"

The atmosphere in the room cooled instantly. "I don't know who my real parents are," he said. "I'm adopted."

"Oh." Sarah flushed with irritation at her own persistence. She struggled to think of something acceptable to say. "Have you ever tried to find them?"

His voice assumed a measure of contempt. "My mother's dead . . . my real mother, I mean. She killed herself after I was born. She didn't even know who my father was. One of hundreds, probably."

"But your adoptive parents . . . ," Sarah floundered, ". . . they've been good to you?"

He turned his back to her, the music ebbing, the delicate fabric between them tearing away. She had crossed the line of intimacy.

Unzipping the pocket to her knapsack, Sarah produced the bundle of photos. She took Michael's hand and pulled him down on the bed beside her. They sat, shoulders touching, as she went through the photos, rhyming off names, explaining what she knew about the people in them. Except for the girl. She said nothing about her. But he asked about her almost immediately.

"That's my secret," Sarah said, almost in a whisper. "I don't know who she is . . . or why she's there."

"Or what she is," he added pointedly.

"You mean a ghost?" She laughed nervously. "I thought you'd think I was crazy if I suggested it."

He picked up her glass. "Your drink is empty." He walked from the room, leaving her sitting on the bed.

Sarah rewrapped the photos quickly and pushed them into her knapsack. She looked for Michael and found him standing in front of the sink, ice cube tray in hand. The rest of the house was clean and modest like his room, save for the artifacts that crowded every surface. Masks on walls and stands, a totem pole, weapons, ceremonial garb, feathers, headdresses, dream catchers, beads, jewellery, moccasins, carvings, gloves, photos, bones. His dad's "museum," Michael called it. A closet anthropologist.

"What's he hoping to find?" Sarah asked as she looked at one of the masks.

"A channel to another dimension."

"Come on." Sarah turned to look at him and saw that he was serious.

"There are those who believe that the dream world is the real world," he said. "They believe that this world is an illusion or a trick. My father hopes to pull down the veil between dreams and reality, to open a channel for spirits to break through so that we can communicate."

"You mean, ghosts . . ."

"Not just ghosts. Spirit walkers, travellers, guides."

It all sounded credible when Michael said it, like everyone thought that way. Like it was common knowledge that spirits wandered back and forth between worlds, spending time with the living when they weren't hanging out with the dead. Standing next to beds, boots glistening with mud. "Isn't that a strange philosophy for a medical doctor?" she asked. "I mean, isn't that kind of spiritual voodoo verboten in the scientific community?" She stood in front of an inscrutable red-and-blue face, the eyes striped with white paint like terrible claw marks, the face surrounded in wolf skin, the wolf's muzzle draped over the forehead with two coal-black braids hanging down. "Who's this?"

Michael glanced at the mask. "A Cheyenne warrior. The cavalry called them dog soldiers. They were an elite group of the strongest and the bravest in the tribe. They were mean mothers, fighting as rearguards and sacrificial decoys so the rest of the tribe could escape."

Now it was her turn to look at him with amusement. "Do you always talk like an encyclopedia?"

He shrugged.

Sarah had to laugh. "You know lots of stuff," she said. "Anyway, it's you. Dog Soldier. That's how I'll think of you from now on." She looked around the room. Over every door was some kind of symbol painted on wood.

He followed her gaze. "Hex craft. It's supposed to protect the house from evil spirits."

"Sounds like witchcraft."

"Actually, they're love charms," he answered snidely, "designed to beguile young women into submitting to my will." He dropped ice cubes into the glasses, glugged rum overtop, the ice cracking in protest. Tipping the bottle to his lips, he drank easily, like he did it all the time, his Adam's apple bobbing up and down. He turned to her and held the bottle to her lips, the amber fire pouring down her throat until she pushed his hand away at last, rum spilling over her mouth. They emptied their glasses in quick shots, discarded them in the sink and took turns from the bottle instead. Stumbling through the living room, Sarah pulled a blue mask with a lolling scarlet tongue from its stand and held it in front of her face. "I am Fire Water, Magic Tongue. Kiss me or die."

He took the mask from her and replaced it. He nudged her against the wall, pressing his body into hers. She could feel his breath against her face. The dusky gleam of half-closed eyes, dark lashes glistening, her heart skipping uncontrollably. She wanted him to kiss her, wanted to feel his mouth against hers.

"Come on, I have something to show you," he said.

Leading her outside, he gestured to the sky where the moon was rising as bloody and monstrous as a vanquished king, its great vermilion face eternally frozen in horrified betrayal. Reflected in his eyes, two miniature red orbs made Michael seem like a demon lover. He held her hand, his warmth, the rum seducing her.

"Someone lit the moon on fire," he said.

"My brains are full of gum," she whispered.

He pulled her down the hill, tripping over rocks and tufts of grass, the night swallowing their laughter, the moon gaping. He towed her along behind him, her hand in his, tugging her through the parking lot to the place where the little fair stood, closed, abandoned, prettier in the crimson light, the maze of hydro wires casting shadowy webs over the buildings and the ground.

"What are you doing?" she asked, giggling.

He worked the lock on one of the buildings, more like a trailer, and the door opened with a creak. He drew her into the darkness, her sneakers squeaking on the floor.

"I can't see."

He pulled her through. He knew the way. Pushing her into the centre of the room, he cast a spell with butane and she saw herself and him, reflected infinitely in the mirrors, like some crone's trick.

"My God," was all she could say.

He conjured a small candle from his pocket, lit it, and a million little flames magically appeared. Taking her hand in his, he used a pen to draw a spiral in blue ink on her palm. "For life," he said, kissing her at last, his mouth warm and lingering.

CHapter Four

The curtains billowed languidly in the morning breeze, the window to Sarah's room still half open, the screen leaning against the wall where she had left it the night before. She'd snuck through the window, not out of fear of her mother, but in honour of him. He was there with her, the smell of him, his hair, his skin, the sound of his voice. Her mind danced like a honeybee when she thought of the night, their reflected images stretching endlessly before them like an augury. She wanted to be with him, wanted to feel his hands against her skin again.

If only she hadn't drunk so much. She massaged her forehead methodically then reached for the aspirin bottle. She would have to take a double dose today. One for the drink and one for her old friend, the migraine. But she didn't regret a minute of it. After all, she'd been so out of it she'd managed to climb into bed without thinking about John's ghost. For that, she was grateful. There had been one moment, though, when she'd thought she saw something move across the threshold of her room. But she hadn't allowed herself to care. And if it was John, he had thankfully left her alone. In the comfort of her bed, with the sunlight streaming through the window and the scent of Michael's skin on her own, she felt she could be hopeful.

Rolling over to reach the aspirin on the milk crate, she hesitated as the floorboards creaked outside her bedroom door. There was a brief pause, then the creaking resumed and receded as her mother finally trundled by, the odour of cigarette smoke attending her like a shadow. Sarah waited for her mother to settle back in to sleep the morning away.

She looked around the room, at the signature of it, the books, posters, clothes and the leaves—lots of leaves everywhere, push-pinned to the corkboard, arranged on top of shelves. There wasn't room for anything or anyone else. She had made sure of that, filling up all the spaces, arranging it neatly. Like an old widow, she had blocked the world out, living in a house too big for her dwindling emotional income, shutting off rooms in her heart that she could no longer afford to heat. No wonder she'd been seeing things. But then Michael had come. Now the curtains waved invitingly; the breeze slipped through the open window, fingering loose papers and leaves, offering a new order. Wasn't Michael just like that, entering her life, rearranging things? The strange thing was that she wanted him to, wanted him to sweep the dust from the corners, to shake things loose. She had been holding on so tightly, hadn't she forgotten why or even how to let go?

The blue ink spiral he had drawn on her hand winked from her palm. "For life," he had said. And so it seemed to be true, that life had a way of asserting itself, reinventing itself, of taking an unexpected turn and springing up in the most unlikely places—in alleyways, beneath uprooted trees, in the cracks of sidewalks, in the palm of your hand. *So does death*, she abruptly thought. Touching the spiral with her finger, she flexed her hand to see it jump in and out. John had seemingly broken through to her world. But Michael had thrown the door wide, offering promise like spring rain. And she was amazed at her own thirst.

The breeze lifted a fan of leaves from her dresser, whirled them to the centre of the room and dropped them in a scatter across the blue-and-green cotton rug that covered the trap door leading to the basement. The trap door. It took up most of her room, causing her to keep her bed shoved against the wall by the window and her dresser pushed against the other wall by the door. Little usable space. She hadn't minded the trap door being in her room before except that she worried it wasn't stable. Just a piece of plywood dropped into the two-by-four frame, no hinges. Looking at it now, Sarah realized how easy it would be for someone to crawl into her room. All they had to do was break a window in the basement and come up the stairs from inside. It would be best to just nail the door shut. There was no reason to go down there anyway. There were hookups for a washer and dryer, but they weren't going to get those any time soon. They used the laundromat down the street.

Sarah suddenly noticed the note, folded into a neat little tent card sitting next to her photo. *"Pushover."* Donna's handwriting. How had she left it there, and when? "God, Donna!" Sarah said aloud, the bedsprings in the next room answering noisily, then growing silent again. She got up from bed and stuffed her legs into her jeans, the pain pulsing firmly at the back of her eyes. Her black turtleneck caused her hair to jump and spark as she pulled it over her head, making her way from the room.

Flipping the light on in the bathroom, she turned the hot water tap in the sink. After testing the temperature with her hand, she splashed water on her face. Her skin turned red with the heat before she resigned herself to showering instead. It would make her late for school, but no matter. It was Friday. Half the seniors wouldn't show up for class. They skipped school to drink. They had the shirts to prove it: "FEWD," for "Forget Education, We're Drinking." Not that she ran with that crowd any more. She avoided them; she didn't want anything to do with their type. Besides, Donna wouldn't allow it. She had made that quite clear. She hated those pricks with their stupid drinking club, she said—and their stupid matching shirts. She was going to have her own shirt made: "FU2."

The pipes to the tub rattled and thumped as the water coughed out, brown with rust. They knocked with diminishing frequency, like a dying drummer, until the water finally ran clear. The steam rose up, a genie in the cool air, filling the tub and eventually the room. Sarah stripped down, kicking her jeans with one foot to the corner of the bathroom. Stepping gingerly into the shower, she let the water rush over her, the temperature almost too hot to bear, then freezing. "Don't use the water!" she yelled into the mist.

There was a light tap on the door. And then another. Sarah depressed the shower lever with her big toe to stop the water so she could hear. Her mother's thin voice mumbled through the door. *Why does she always mumble?*

"What?" Sarah shouted back.

"Telephone. It's the school."

Sarah opened the door a crack, clutching a towel around

her. Her mother's disembodied hand thrust the receiver through.

"Hello . . ."

An angry voice shouted on the other end. "We won't tolerate your tardiness any longer. If you insist on thumbing your nose at school policy we have no choice but to expel you."

"You got me out of the shower, Donna, you jerk!"

Cackling laughter seared through the line, followed by the click and buzz as the phone was disconnected. Sarah tossed the handset back into the kitchen. "Donna's a stupid jerk!" she wrote in the fog on the mirror, her finger squeaking against the glass. When she was finished writing, she wiped the words away with her palm and found John's face staring back at her.

Sarah gave a terrified shout, whipping around to face him. The mist hung in the air, drifting languidly across the bathroom toward the gap where the door was ajar. She kicked angrily at the door, letting the steam escape into the kitchen. Whatever ghosts were there had evaporated with the mist.

Turning back to the mirror, she studied the room in its reflection. Her clothes in a heap on the floor, the shower curtain scrunched to one side, the tub vacant. The possibility that she had imagined the whole thing crept into a corner of her consciousness and curled up there. John beside the bed. His reflection in the mirror. It was stress causing these visions, she told herself. Stress, squeezing the synapses in her brain, fabricating phantoms from little more than misdirected chemicals. It could do that so easily, she knew, fracture the eggshell integrity of the mind. And she had been under stress lately—lots of it. More than one person could bear. She covered her face with her hands and hung her head. "Please, God," she prayed.

The sudden notion that he was somehow still there, watching her, devoured her self-pity in an instant. She wrapped a towel tightly around herself, snapped her clothes from the floor, glanced furtively in the mirror, then trotted quickly to her room, where she dumped her clothes in a bundle at the foot of her bed—though not before checking underneath. Pulling on a clean pair of underwear and her jeans, she unwrapped the towel from around her chest, scrubbed her hair dry, threw on a bra and the black turtleneck from before, swapped the turtleneck for a hooded sweatshirt and put on her jean jacket. After combing her hair until it was straight, she grabbed her green knit toque and pushed her hair up underneath before daring to inspect herself in the round vanity mirror above her dresser. Her grim reflection stared back at her. She spun around sharply to make sure that she was alone, then turned back to the mirror and challenged John to show his face again. "Don't be a coward," she said. When he didn't appear, she grimaced at herself, applied lip gloss and searched her drawer for socks. There was a thin blue pair without holes. She yanked them on quickly, slung her knapsack over one shoulder and her purse over the other. She checked her pockets for money. Ten dollars. Shoving her feet into her sneakers, she popped two aspirins before throwing the bottle into her purse and slamming out of the house toward school. Anything was better than being at home.

✳   ✳   ✳

The hallways were empty, the students already in class. Sarah felt exhausted and the pain in her head was growing. Her feet dragged as she climbed the seemingly endless marble stairs to the third floor. Stair after stair. How many stairs had she climbed in her life? There had been many. Maybe enough to climb to the moon. She used to count them, when counting was all she had to keep herself sane.

The Terrace General Hospital had 29 terrazzo stairs between floors, for a total of 87 steps—minus landings—to reach the chronic care ward in the west wing on the third floor. There were two sets of elevators, only one of which worked on a regular basis, the second having fallen into disrepair when budget cuts apparently prevented regular maintenance from being performed. It took 162 steps to reach the stairwell from the main floor lobby, with an additional 412 steps and three right turns to reach the wire-reinforced glass doors leading to the chronic care wing. Once through the doors, a total of 69 steps were necessary to reach the nurses' station, 94 to reach the showers, 108 to reach the linen closet and 258 to reach Room 319, with another 17½ steps to reach the bed from the doorway, the half step a compromise between the floor and the edge of the bed. Room 319 was a single-occupancy facility, a rarity in chronic care wards, with a wide dusty window overlooking the hospital atrium—a square of weeds and forgotten flower beds, no seats. Rooms facing south overlooked the cemetery.

Donna was waiting for her in the hall outside of class, striking a pose against the green-painted cinderblock wall, brown plaid kilt cut just below her crotch, black boots to the knee, one foot kicked up behind her buttock. Sarah walked past like she didn't know her.

"Don't even think about it, Wagner. You're late anyway. You'll just get a detention."

Sarah sighed. "Why do you torment me so?"

"If I didn't, who would? Come on. The Queen's calls."

Sarah didn't want to go. She wanted to see Michael. But Donna was right. She would only get a detention if she entered class this late. Donna tromped down the school steps, towing Sarah along behind her.

"Man, did you miss out last night," she gloated as they reached the street. "A bunch of us went to hear this great band at the Southside Hotel."

"Who's a bunch of us?"

"Peter and some friends from out of town."

"Oh, right, Peter." Sarah didn't have the energy to fake enthusiasm.

"But these guys show up," Donna continued, "and they're making like they own the place, you know, ordering all these drinks and taking up all the good seats, stealing chairs from our table, talking big, and the next thing you know, Peter's friend grabs one of these guys and nearly splits his head open with a head butt, and then everybody's fighting and smashing beer bottles."

Sarah looked skeptical. "Peter?"

"You should have seen him!" Donna said, becoming more animated. "I'm just sitting there when the waiter throws his tray across the room and slams these two guys right on top of our table. I jump out of the way and nearly get suckered by this freak, but Peter dives on the guy and punches him out."

"Sounds like a great time."

"Don't be a bitch. It was a riot."

"Literally . . . I can't see Peter fighting."

"Oh, he can fight," Donna assured her. "There's lots of stuff you don't know about him."

"I can live with that." Sarah leaned on the door to the coffee shop and stumbled inside to the thick smell of deep-fried food and the haze of cigarette smoke. Moving to their usual booth at the back of the shop, she dumped her knapsack on the seat, then squeezed in beside it. Donna sat across from her.

"Okay, so give me the scoop," she said.

"What do you mean?" Sarah asked. She searched Donna's face for a clue as to what was coming.

"Come on, Wagner. You've been out to lunch lately, day-dreaming and getting all pissy about everything. What's going on?"

"I don't know," Sarah said, shrugging. "It's this headache. It won't go away." She dug for the aspirin in her bag.

"Go see a doctor," Donna suggested, producing a bottle of Advil and tossing it across the table.

Sarah scowled. "No! No doctors. I'll never see another doctor again, I don't care what's wrong with me. They can't help anybody." She shook two Advil from the bottle and slid it back to Donna. "Thanks," she said in a calmer voice.

Donna dropped the bottle in her purse and tapped a couple of cigarettes from her pack. She lit both at once with her Zippo and handed one to Sarah. Sarah took a deep drag, exhaled appreciatively and looked around the shop. There were several people scattered around at tables and in booths. Dishes clattered in the kitchen as Nick called out orders, coffee cups settled into saucers, lighters sparked, cigarettes glowed, newspapers rustled beneath the low groan of comfort while a middle-aged waitress skimmed adeptly along with dishcloth and coffee carafe synchrony, her dirty blond hair and expression moulded to withstand the smoke and grease and demands of the patrons. Sarah settled back into the booth. It was a relief to be there after all, playing her part in this small theatre of life. Taking another long drag on her cigarette, she slowly exhaled. "I'm sorry, Donna. I guess I've been freaking out."

Donna considered her through hooded eyes. "Over what?"

"I don't know." Sarah picked the foil from the cigarette pack and began folding it into smaller and smaller triangles. "I think I'm seeing things."

"Does it start with an *M* and end with an *L*?" Donna smiled patronizingly behind her cigarette.

"I'm serious," Sarah said, furrowing her brow. "I'm kind of scared."

"Scared of what? You haven't told me anything yet."

Sarah looked into Donna's face. Beneath the shock of short black hair, her eyes shone green and clear, her unnaturally large pupils the size of nickels in the light of the diner. It gave her a nocturnal, otherworldly quality—almost trance-like, Sarah thought, raising the cigarette to her lips. As she did this, she felt a warm fluid run down her finger. It exploded in a brilliant red starburst onto the table.

"Sarah, your nose!"

Sarah drew her hand from her face. Her fingers were crimson with blood. "Shit."

Donna reached for the napkins and pulled a handful from the dispenser. "Here, pinch your nose with these."

Dropping her cigarette in the ashtray, Sarah grabbed the napkins from Donna's hand and crammed them over her nose, tilting her head back.

"God, that was weird," Donna said, pulling more napkins

from the dispenser. "Maybe you should go to the bathroom and check it out."

The napkins blossomed red as Sarah slid across the booth. In the bathroom, she removed them cautiously and inspected her nose. The bleeding seemed to have stopped. There was a smear of blood above her lip and her fingers were sticky with it. Turning on the tap, she rubbed her hands vigorously under the water, then leaned over and repeatedly splashed her face. She did this until the red-tinted water ran clear down the drain. Using a wad of paper towels, she dabbed her face delicately, afraid her nose would start to bleed again if she used too much force. When she was satisfied that the bleeding had stopped, she opened her compact and applied powder heavily. She surveyed her face in the mirror. Her skin was pale and malnourished looking. Dark circles like tea-coloured stains had crept into the hollows below her eyes. She looked tired and worn out. And somehow thinner. Why hadn't she noticed that before? It was a good thing she hadn't gone to school today. What if the nose bleed had happened in front of the whole class? In front of Michael? She found her lipstick and dotted some on her cheeks, blending it into her skin. At least she wouldn't look so pale now. After fussing with her hair for a bit, she threw the blood-stained napkins in the garbage and went back out. She was going to tell Donna about John.

"Hey, look who I found," Donna said, grabbing Sarah by the hand and drawing her into the booth. Peter smiled happily back at her.

"What a coincidence," Sarah mumbled. She forced a smile. "Hey, Peter."

"I was just telling her all about the fun she missed last night," Donna said to Peter.

"How's your nose?" Peter asked.

Sarah drew her hand self-consciously to her face. "Oh, it's fine," she said, frowning at Donna.

Donna laughed, waving her off with her cigarette. "It happens every twenty-eight days like clockwork."

"Big party at my place," Peter reminded Sarah. "You're gonna be there, right?"

"Of course she is," Donna jumped in. "We're coming together, if you know what I mean." Donna and Peter snickered conspiratorially.

They had the same kind of teeth, Sarah noticed, jagged and pointy, like a couple of sharks, or grinning jack-o'-lanterns.

He turned to her. "Bring your guitar, Sarah. We can play a few tunes."

"Uh . . . I don't know, Peter . . ." she said, tapping absently at the numbers on the small jukebox on the table. She spun the dial and watched as the music selections fell one on top of the other in a metallic fan.

"Come on. You're great," Peter persisted.

Donna winked at Sarah. "That's what all the boys say."

Just then, the bell on the door jangled angrily and a dozen or more students burst loudly into the coffee shop wearing matching red-and-white-striped jerseys with "FEWD" across the chest.

"Oh God," Donna spat. "What are they doing here?" She glared across the diner as the group took up several booths and started yelling out orders to the waitress. Snatching a quarter from a pile of change on the table, Donna leaned over and forced the coin into the jukebox, then punched a number in, cranking the volume knob as high as it would go. Nirvana's "Territorial Pissings" screamed out. "It's pricks like that that give us students a bad name," she said with a feigned British accent. She grabbed the Zippo and began snapping it aggressively, open and shut.

"They're not all bad," Peter said.

Sarah shot Donna a pointed look: *What do you think of him now?*

Nick sauntered up to the table, apparently wearing the same filthy apron, his belly seemingly bigger. "You order or you leave."

"When's it due?" Donna snorted into her hand. She smacked another cigarette from the pack and lit it. Still affecting the accent, she spoke through a cloud of smoke. "I'll have toast and marmalade with a spot of coffee. Oh, and Nick, old man . . . could you be a dear and tell that group of rowdies to keep it down over there? We're trying to have a conversation." She raised her eyebrows and picked at her teeth with her black-polished nails.

"Whatta you want?" Nick said, ignoring Donna's request and pointing his pen at Peter and Sarah.

"Same."

"Same."

Their orders arrived, and Sarah sipped the morning away with her coffee. There would be no seeing Michael today, she concluded, not with Donna on duty. She would have to hang with her throughout the day and into the night. Maybe even Peter, too. She would bide her time until she could slip away, then sneak over to Michael's later. She definitely didn't want to go home, not with John potentially waiting there. But she would have to put in a good show to avoid suspicion or Donna might follow her around all night. She knew she could wait it out. She'd done it often enough before.

61

Hospital time was different than ordinary time. It had landmarks, but no destinations. Morning meds, 7:00 am. Breakfast, 7:30 am. Tray pickup at 9:15. Sponge bath and fresh linen, 10:30. Noon meds, 11:00 am. Lunch, 12 noon, and so on, until lights out at 9:00 pm. It was the nighttime that got especially difficult, with its liquid edges and confused intentions. Nighttime was for sleeping, though sleep rarely arrived to claim those delinquent hours. And so it was spent listening and waiting, the minutes placed end to end and stretching out toward eternity.

"So what do you want to do?" Peter asked.

Donna looked at him suggestively. "What are you offering?"

"We could go to my place."

"And . . ."

"Blow a few, if you want . . ."

"Definitely want."

"What about you, Sarah?" Peter asked.

"Oh, she's in," Donna answered for her.

Sarah lowered her eyes. "Yeah, sure, let's go."

"Okay," Peter said, a little too excitedly. Pulling a wad of money from his pocket, he made a big show of picking up the tab, peeling off several bills with quick snaps.

Trying to earn brownie points, Sarah thought, disdainfully.

The three of them got up from the table and walked across the shop together.

"Hey, look! Candy canes!" Donna chimed as they moved past FEWD territory.

Insults and wadded-up napkins flew through the air.

"Hey, Peter! Whatta you doing with that scag?" someone called out.

"Get bit," Donna called back, flicking her cigarette butt at one of the tables.

"Thanks, Donna." Sarah pulled up the collar on her jean jacket and dodged a napkin bomb. She pushed open the door and stepped into the autumn afternoon, the air refreshingly crisp and clear after the smoky haze of the coffee shop.

Donna came shrieking out to the sidewalk. Lifting her kilt, she mooned the coffee shop window. "That's the most they'll get tonight."

"Doubtful," Sarah muttered. She stood with Donna in front of the shop while Peter hung back, talking to some friends. Donna knocked on the glass, made a face at him. He raised his hand, indicating he'd only be a moment. Donna knocked louder, until Nick's irate face appeared in the doorway.

"You get outta here!" he yelled.

"You get outta here!" Donna yelled back, copying his accent.

"Jeez, Donna." Sarah shook her head.

Nick jabbed his arm rudely in the air. Donna did the same until Peter squeezed past the gesticulating Nick and out the door. He put his arms around Donna and Sarah, Donna talking loudly, singing, making people look. Peter squeezed Sarah's shoulder, laughing. *Dream on.* Sarah turned away just in time to see Michael stepping out of the arcade at the end of the block. He squinted down at her from the doorway and watched them walk by. Watched her walk by. Their eyes met, his opinion obvious. Donna grabbed the back of Peter's pants as they passed and stuck her tongue out at Michael. Sarah averted her eyes to the sidewalk; she'd have to explain later. Tugging the hat playfully from Sarah's head, Donna put it on her own as Sarah squirmed to get away from Peter, who only pulled her closer.

* * *

They stood outside the club, a line of people shifting like zombies behind them, drawn to the same place without knowing why. The music throbbed through the walls, blaring when the black-painted door opened, dampening when it slammed shut.

"They're friends of mine," Peter yelled to the bouncer as the door opened again. "Sarah plays a little guitar." He moved his fingers like he was playing a heavy riff so the bouncer would understand him.

Sarah covered her mouth with one hand to keep from bursting out in derisive laughter. The bouncer nodded sternly at her. Looked at her chest. The music swallowed them as they pushed their way in, the crowd seething, surging, parting, fusing together. Peter's face so close to hers.

"What do you think?" he shouted.

"They have to be breaking some kind of fire regulation," she yelled back. "All these people . . ."

"Yeah, on fire!" he said. He put his arm around her again and waved to his friends as if to say, "Look who I'm here with." He turned to kiss her, trying to cop a feel under her jean jacket.

Sarah pushed him away. "I need a beer," she said, pointing at her throat. "I'm so dry."

Peter disappeared on a quest for beer. Sarah shoved through the crowd, past men looking fierce, looking hopeful. The room swaying, faces blurring. The music pressing against her, into her head, pounding to the rhythm of the pain thumping in her temples. Someone grabbed her. It was

Donna, dragging her toward the washroom and the glare of fluorescent lights.

"Look what I found," she said, placing a little white pill into her hand. "Merry Christmas."

Sarah shook her head, stumbled into a bathroom stall, slammed the door and locked it.

"Come out and dance with me," Donna said. "Don't be a drag, Wagner. You're being such a drag." She banged on the door, kicked it, waited, then finally left, the music surging and receding as the bathroom door opened and closed.

Sitting on the edge of the toilet, Sarah made up her mind to ditch Peter and Donna both, now that she could slip out unnoticed. She flushed the pill and left the bathroom.

But Peter was waiting for her outside the door with a pint of beer. He handed her the glass and leaned toward her, slobbering against her face. She took a gulp of beer, spilling most of it trying to dodge Peter's groping mouth, and thought she would scream.

"Could you hold this for a minute?" she said, sloshing the beer against his chest. Before he could figure out what was going on, she squeezed through the crowd and bolted through the rear exit into the alley, where she started to run. Afraid he would follow her, she kept running until she was over the bridge toward the park, slowing down only when she reached the stand of pine trees, the cool air helping to clear her head. Over the night-washed landscape, the moon was strapped to the sky by the crisscross of hydro wires, the forked path up the hill like frozen lightning in the grass. It pointed to the little house hiding beneath the spruce trees, one eye open. His room.

Creeping up to the house, Sarah stood on the stone and

peeked through the glass. The light was on but the room was empty. She walked around the house, gaping through the darkened windows, the accusatory faces of the masks gaping back at her. "I can't go home," she said aloud, making her way back to his room. Standing on the stone again, she could see that the window was slightly ajar. A small push and it swished easily open. She measured her options briefly, then clambered up, feet kicking against the side of the house, the sill cutting into her hips until she flopped onto the bed like a fish.

Unsure of what to do, she simply lay there, her ears still ringing from the noise in the bar. What if his father came home? It would be best to leave, to pretend she was never there. But she didn't want to go. She felt she had to see him or she would go crazy. *More crazy.* The pot and alcohol helped influence her decision to stay, encouraging her to put her head down on the pillow and wait for him to crawl in beside her. It was too tempting to explore, though, to see more of him. She got up slowly and moved over to the shelves.

The stacks of videos sat neatly filed next to the TV. Each one had a clean white label bearing only the date, nothing more. Sarah selected one: January 8. She looked at it and pushed it into the machine. Turning on the TV, she adjusted the volume so there was no sound. The tape rolled and jumped. There was no image, only snow. Then the faint outline of a young child. A boy, maybe? Michael? A cousin, running along the beach? The picture was grainy, uncertain. Now the boy walked down the hallway of an old house, opening doors, the rooms cavernous and uninviting. The image cut to a dog, a golden retriever, trotting along a sidewalk, looking into the camera, a thin cord of silver trailing behind it like a luminescent spiderweb. The screen blurred with snow as the picture skipped away.

The fog buzzed on the screen for a while before Sarah decided there was nothing else on the tape and rewound it. Putting it carefully back in its jacket, she replaced the tape on the shelf in its original spot and selected another: July 15. Again the blurred image, the tape jumping, but the same boy, it seemed. As she checked the date on the jacket again, a strange cityscape sprang up on the screen, the buildings slightly distorted, sometimes looming, sometimes wavering as though under water. Then nothing, the image fading to static. Sarah hit rewind, replaced the tape and pushed another into the machine: September 15. The tape was blurry, as before, the image snapping and jumping. But this time the figure of a woman slowly emerged. A young woman with long hair, sitting on the edge of a bed. The aspect of the room was familiar. It was Michael's room, she realized, yet somehow different, with certain details more vivid than others, while other parts receded into shadow. The camera moved closer to the girl, her face in profile and indistinct, the features unclear except for the smile that crept across her face as she let her jacket slip from her shoulders and worked the edge of her sweater up, her long hair fanning out, her breasts blooming from beneath the sweater, exposed and full, like peonies.

Sarah giggled, she couldn't help herself. *So this is your secret.*

The girl laughed too, her face turned away for a long while before she finally faced the camera, the image flickering, becoming cloudy, then starkly sharp. Sarah gasped.

"What are you doing here?"

She spun around in horror as Michael's silhouette filled the doorway, the image of the girl still moving on the screen.

"What—what is this?" she stammered, pointing at the screen.

He glanced at the TV. "Turn it off. I can explain."

The girl in the tape continued to laugh, inching her jeans down over her hips.

"How did you do this?" Sarah shrieked, finding her voice. "How did you get this tape of me?"

Michael moved toward her, catching her wrists as her fists flew up to his face, beating wildly. "Listen to me. It isn't real."

"Get away from me!" she screamed. She fell away from him, grabbed her bag and shoved past him, through the door and into the living room, where the masks loomed.

"Sarah, please let me explain!"

Struggling with the lock, she flung the door open and ran into the night. Her knees gave way as she slipped on the wet grass and stumbled down the hill. Without looking back, she picked herself up and continued to run, her hair whipping around her face, the tears stinging her eyes. She could hear him at the top of the hill, calling her name through the dark.

CHaPTer FIVe

The oak tree shimmered with yellow and gold leaves. She had been walking toward it when she registered a sound, creeping into her slumbering consciousness, barely brushing the edge of audibility. It started low, like it was coming from somewhere in the bowels of the house, then working its way up through the damp concrete foundation and into the floorboards. It found its way into her room and, miraculously, to the receptors in her dreaming ears, forcing her awake. It grew gradually louder and more urgent. *The cry of a baby.* Where was it coming from? Someone had left their infant outside, obviously. Outside in the cold. Sarah eyed the rug over the trap door fearfully. She willed the parents to pick the baby up, to stop it from crying. But when its wails grew louder and more wrenching still, she covered her ears with her hands. Someone should do something. *Someone should make it stop.* And then it did, the wails reduced to a muffled whimpering as if someone had pushed a pillow over the child's red little face.

✻   ✻   ✻

Sarah wasn't at all comfortable. Sitting on the couch, wedged between two men she didn't know, a drink clasped desperately in her hands, the ice melting in clear, limpid spirals into the rust-coloured brandy in her glass. Who were these guys, anyway? Too old to be at some high school party, that was clear. Lest they think she was interested, Sarah stared straight ahead, careful not to engage them with so much as a glance. Donna danced wildly in front of her, surrounded by a group of admirers, enjoying the attention.

Sarah gulped her drink, her stomach bucking with the kick of nausea. But no matter how much she drank or how sick she felt, she couldn't stop thinking about Michael, about the video she'd seen. Tilting her glass back recklessly, she spilled the brandy down her chin and onto her shirt.

"Drink much?" the guy beside her yelled over the music.

Sarah didn't flinch, didn't so much as look at him. *To look into an insane man's eyes is to share his insanity*. Isn't that what Donna was always saying? She wiped her chin with her sleeve and stared into her glass. Somehow last night had become tonight. She had blurred through the entire day and into this evening. Had she even sobered up from the night before? She couldn't remember much of anything except fumbling toward sleep and narrowly missing it, her mind staggering in and out of consciousness, the oak tree looming in her dozing state. And the baby crying. She remembered that. Now she was here, at Peter's party. He'd looked happy to see her when she arrived, even though she'd run out on him. "A bad trip," she'd said. He seemed to accept that. Certainly, it had nothing to do with him.

The worst part, the part that kept her drinking, was that she really liked Michael—and that Donna was apparently right. Maybe he was just a wanker. But what had he meant when he'd said the video wasn't real? She drained her glass, then stood up shakily and moved into the crowd. Donna pulled her into the throbbing dance.

"It's Nirvana, it's 'Breed'," she shouted.

"I know," Sarah shouted back. She danced half-heartedly, Donna's face inches from her own, laughing maniacally. One of the boys put his arms around Sarah's waist, tried to dirty dog her. Another lurched toward her, pointing at Donna.

"She's something else, huh?"

"Yeah," Sarah yelled into his ear. "Too bad she's gay!" She raised her eyebrows and nodded at the guy to show that she was serious, enjoying his look of shock.

She pushed her way into the kitchen. There were people standing everywhere, leaning on counters, sitting on top of the table, going through the fridge. She had to reach through a group of leering guys to get the mickey of cherry brandy she'd hid inside the flour canister. The alcohol splashed from the bottle, Sarah pouring until her glass was half full. Closing the cap, she went to replace it inside the canister, then decided against it and slipped the bottle into her jacket just as Peter appeared. He picked her up, slung her over his shoulder and wheeled her around, the brandy flying in loose ribbons from her glass. In spite of herself, she shrieked and laughed, the bluegrass tumbler slipping from her hand and falling end over end through the air. She couldn't stop Peter, couldn't stop herself laughing, her ribs aching from the effort. He carried her through the house, toward the door.

"Come for a walk with me," he said as he dropped her to her feet in the hall.

Sarah turned away from him.

"Come for a walk with me," he said again, moving closer to her.

His features faded in a fog of alcohol as she tried to focus on his face, marvelling that he carried two tiny lamps where his pupils should be. And then she saw Michael, standing across the hall, watching her. She leaned toward Peter, pulled him closer and put her mouth on his. Michael was suddenly beside them, yanking Peter away from her. "Don't do that," he said.

"Hey, get lost, buddy!" Peter wrenched his sleeve from Michael's hand. Michael stood a good foot taller. He looked at Sarah, his face set with anger.

"Leave me alone," she groaned.

"You heard her, pal. Leave her alone." Peter shoved Michael's chest and turned to Sarah.

Michael grabbed Peter's shirt, pulling him easily backwards. Peter knocked Michael's hand away. "I said get lost! This is a closed party."

"Keep your hands off her."

There was a lightning pop as Peter swung and missed, striking Michael's shoulder. Michael clenched Peter's shirt at the throat, his fist thumping like a jackrabbit until Peter crashed to the floor, blood and spit fanning out through the air. Peter covered his ears with his hands as Michael's boots connected again and again, the rage surging as the boys from the party tore in like dogs let loose, howling. Reaching for Sarah's hand, Michael tugged her through the door. They slipped across the grass, voices shouting after them, growing fainter as they ducked down an alley, breathless and running, crashing over garbage cans.

They ran through the half-lit streets, Michael pulling Sarah along beside him until they reached the bridge. Half-

way across, he stopped and released her hand. Sarah dou-
bled over, struggling to breathe, the pain detonating in her
head, the night spinning around her, streaked with stars.

"You're crazy," she blurted out. "He won't forget that any
time soon."

"I don't care."

"I mean it. He's a big prick." She stood up, the world right-
ing itself, the gyre in her head grinding slowly down. "I
shouldn't even be talking to you. What were you doing
there?" She eyed him angrily, secretly hoping it was for her.

"I was looking for you. I want to show you something."

"I don't want to see any more videos."

"You have to let me explain."

And then they were standing in front of his house.
Michael opened the door with the gold key. "In case my old
man's home," he said.

He walked through the rooms, snapping on lights, calling
out for his father.

The masks stared silently back.

"Is he ever home?" Sarah asked.

"No. Almost never. But he has a weird way of showing up
when I don't want him to."

"Like, when you're making porn videos?"

He looked at her, a pained expression on his face. "Come
here." He took her hand and led her down the hall to his bedroom.

Sarah hesitated at the door.

"Trust me," he said. Turning on the light, he guided her to
the yellow upholstered chair and made her sit. He stood
before her as in confession. "I had a dream about you—after
the first time I saw you, a couple of weeks before school
started. I dreamt about you, like that, on my bed. "

"Oh God," Sarah moaned. "Donna was right . . ."

"So then I made you real. I found your picture in the year-book. I got it out of the library. I used animation software to graft your face onto a video clip I pulled off the net, used more software to put you on my bed . . ."

Sarah held her head in her hands. "It isn't normal to do things like that, Michael," she said, talking to the carpet. "It's weird. It's the kind of stuff you read about in the papers."

"In my own defence," Michael said, "'normal' is a very loosely defined label." He smiled, raising his eyebrows hope-fully. "I didn't do it out of disrespect," he continued. "I thought if I made it real, one of two things would happen."

"What's that?" Sarah asked flatly.

"Either I'd find you in my bed one day . . . or I'd secure a job for myself as the king of custom pornography."

"Sounds like a future," she said wryly. But even as she said it, she could feel herself forgiving him. After all, was it so wrong for him to want her? "How many other girls have you 'animated'?"

"Just you. It's only ever been you. I'm not a total creep."

Sarah broke down and smiled. She liked him too much to believe that he was all bad. "The other videos I saw . . ."

"Just a boy whose pictures I found. I've been fooling around with old photos for years. Come on, I'll show you."

Selecting a video from the stack on his shelf, he pushed it into the VCR and turned on the TV. The video popped and jumped. The image of a small boy came into view, strolling along a beach. The boy stopped to pick up a stone, threw it into the ocean, the water radiating out in concentric circles where the stone hit the water. A rush of stars and moons and planets sprang spontaneously from the spot where the stone landed, the stars streaking across the screen, then travelling

74

backwards, folding into the water, the ocean disappearing down a funnel with the moons and planets, until there was a single drop of water that blossomed and pulsed like the translucent heart of a developing fetus, floating in the black of space.

He turned to her, his face lit with a strange ecstasy.

"It's beautiful," she said.

He moved over to his desk and sat in the chair. Rolling the mouse, he clicked it and opened a window. "Look. CGI— computer-generated images." He opened several files to show her how it worked. "I create them on the computer, then transfer them to video."

Sarah touched the screen. "Why video? It seems kind of . . . backward."

"I like the quality," Michael explained. "The graininess. The knowledge of the hand and eye behind the camera. It's like people who insist on listening to vinyl. I'm a dedicated video man in the end."

Sarah watched in wonder as the images flashed across the screen in a metonymic stream. "Where did you get the idea for this?"

He stroked his chin thoughtfully as though searching for an answer that would make sense to her. "I've read books about near-death experiences," he said at last. "There are stories of how some people visit rooms filled with frozen images of their own lives that hang in the air like photographs. And when they touch them, the images come to life revealing scenes from their past."

The idea struck a profound chord in Sarah's heart. To see your whole life play out in front of you . . . how long would that take? Seconds? Hours? Days? Was it like watching a film in fast forward? Or was there the opportunity to rewind? At what point in death did this happen? Was there awareness? Emotion? Sensation? Or a kind of clinical detachment? And how big was the gap between living and dying, the dream-crossed twilight before the body was considered dead and the spirit realized that the life it once occupied was gone? It was like the philosophical question Mr. Kovski once posed: If the number of fractions is infinite, can a door ever really close? Was time different for the dying, then? In the moment that it takes for a leaf to fall from a tree, could an entire lifetime be relived? And what of the future? Sarah wondered. Did the dying receive glimpses into that as well?

The questions whirled through her mind until she felt that her head would explode. She looked into Michael's eyes. *Those eyes.* Almost too much to bear, like staring into the sun, his honesty overwhelming her, making her want to break down and weep. He seemed to sense this and pushed his chair away from his desk. Scanning the stack of videos, he pulled the one of Sarah off the shelf and handed it to her. "Here. Take it."

"I guess I kind of freaked out," Sarah said. "It isn't every day that you find a pirate video of your naked self on a strange man's bed."

"You think I'm strange?"

"Yes, I do." She laughed softly, the last of her resolve washing quietly away. "Can I ask you something?" she asked on impulse. "You have to promise you won't make fun of me."

"Okay, I promise."

"I'm serious."

"So am I."

Sarah shifted in her seat, wondering if she was doing the

right thing, then blurted the question out. "Do you think the dead walk among us?"

"What, like zombies?"

"No," she scoffed, as if the idea were far more ridiculous than the one she was about to propose. "Like ghosts, I mean."

"Yeah, sure," he said confidently.

She looked at him warily. "You're not just humouring me?"

"Look around here, Sarah. This house is filled with ghosts." He held her gaze to prove it.

"So, what's your theory?"

"My theory . . ." he said, taking a moment to assemble one. "My theory is that ghosts are psychogenic manifestations of dead people. They're all around us. Some people are just more sensitive to their presence than others, so they see them."

"What do you mean, 'psychogenic'?"

"A creation of the mind."

"So, only crazy people see ghosts, is that what you're saying?"

"No," he said, shaking his head. "Have you always been this paranoid?" He reached over and squeezed her hand when he saw the hurt expression on her face. "I'm sorry, I didn't mean that. I think ghosts appear because people are thinking about that person, that somehow the mind acts as a conduit for the spirit, that's all."

"Oh," she said, regretting her hot-tempered response. It wasn't a bad theory. After all, she did think about John—a lot. In fact, not a day had gone by since he'd left that she hadn't thought about him. Couldn't his appearance in her room be the result of her endless longing to see him again? Of her fathomless grief?

Placing a hand on her cheek, Michael gently turned her face to meet his. "Are you seeing ghosts, Sarah?"

The tears welled in her eyes. "I'm not sure any more," she whispered as he pressed his mouth against her lips, her salty tears mingling with his kisses.

"Stay with me," he said.

CHapTer SIX

The lock on the front door was stiff from the cold. Sarah had to jiggle the key repeatedly before it would turn. It was going to be a tough winter, the man on the radio had said. The *Farmer's Almanac* had predicted it. At last the door swung open. Sarah caught it before it slammed against the wall and closed it quickly so as not to let the cold in. Unbuttoning her coat, she stuffed her mitts in the pockets and hung it on a peg behind the door. She removed her sneakers without untying the laces by stepping on the heels, then pulled her crocheted lime-green slippers over her socks. A dollar store find. They suited her. They were inexpensive and sufficiently dampened the sound of her feet against the floor. Anything to keep her mother from getting up and out of bed.

Sarah shuffled through the darkened living room to the kitchen, reached through the door, groped for the switch and turned the light on. A ghoulish face stared back at her. She shouted. But it was only her mother.

"What are you doing sitting in the dark?" Sarah demanded. It was the most she'd said to her in weeks.

Her mother sat stiffly in her rumpled housecoat, obligatory cigarette in her hand. In front of her, spread out like playing cards, were dozens of photographs. Photographs of John. Sarah stepped down into the kitchen, glaring at the pictures. Were those the photos from the box in her room?

"He was here," her mother croaked.

Sarah looked at her with disgust. She felt little for this woman, this old dishrag of a mother. The thin shadow that she had become, the hands, like claws, the shrunken face, wizened with care and sorrow and disappointment. She'd given up so easily. *Succumbed.* Sarah could see that she was upset, though. The ashtray overflowed with spent butts.

"Who was here?" she asked.

"John!" her mother barked, as though Sarah should have known. "He was here," she said again, "walking through this house." Her hand trembled as she lifted the cigarette to her pinched colourless mouth.

"You couldn't have seen him," Sarah snapped back, but looked instinctively over her shoulder as she walked to the table. *He wouldn't show himself to you,* she thought. *He didn't love you.*

Her ministrations were simply tolerated with quiet dignity, face turned toward the curtained window, arms held limply at either side. Her stupid attempt at comfort, sitting on the edge of the bed dutifully holding the spiritless hand. A miserable Pietà. *And the painting of the deer she'd hung on the wall at the foot of the bed. "Something to look at," she'd said, its deep colours a rich palette for the fanciful mental tapestries stitched by the mind's slow decay. The fantastic mirages spun out like boiled sugar by morphine and hunger, eyes fluttering, pale lips moving in incomprehensible con-*

versations with a procession of friends that paraded end-lessly by, like some demonic masque.

Sarah gathered the photos from the table, as her mother sat, unmoving. "Stay out of my things," she ordered acidly.

"He was here," her mother repeated feebly as Sarah retreated to her room.

※ ※ ※

There was the off chance that the old lady was finally crazy. That they were both crazy. Her mother had her strange ways, her coffee-and-cigarette religion, her mutterings, her loyalty to her bed, her housecoat and slippers that she wore like a uniform. But Sarah never considered for a moment that she would go totally off her nut and actually start hallucinating. *He was here,* she'd insisted. *Why?* Sarah thought angrily. To sift through the remains of spent cigarettes? Cipher the meaning of used coffee grounds in a forgotten cup?

But she had seen him too. She would never tell her mother that—out of spite maybe, or jealousy. Jealous of a ghost. Sarah rejected the idea, trying to stem the wave of fear her mother's admission had caused. Pulling the covers up to her chin, she confessed to herself that she was petrified he would show up again, with his muddy boots and icy hands. She was suddenly panic-stricken by the feeling that she was going to die, that death would root her out tonight, in her sleep. Maybe that's what John was—the angel of death coming for her. Wasn't that how it worked in the movies? Death assumed a friendly face, so it could catch you unawares.

What form had death taken when it appeared to John? She tried to imagine what it had been like for him, wrestling with the certainty of it. "I just don't think about it," he had said, the morphine glazing his eyes. And then, "Could you stay, just until I'm asleep?"

✻   ✻   ✻

It was the sound again, the smothered baby, its plaintive cries resonating clearly in the subconscious rooms of her dreams. Sarah jolted awake, heart pounding, hands clammy with sweat. She held her breath and listened. The furnace kicked to life in the basement, whirring slowly, forcing air to rattle through the heating ducts. It was nothing, she told herself as she slumped in bed, burying her face in her hands.

Before the baby she had been dreaming about John. It was a nice dream. Following him through the woods, moving easily through the trees. The forest murmuring all around them, calling out their names in familiar voices. When John stopped, Sarah realized that they were standing in front of a tree—the oak tree. And then the dream changed. She was shut up in a room without light, the door sealed, the air thick, drawing like warm taffy into her lungs. The baby's high-pitched wails distant and faint, emanating from the bottom of an abandoned well, then growing louder, until it sounded as if the baby were sealed in the room with her. But it wasn't a baby. It was the sound of a woman crying.

"Shhhit," Sarah hissed. The familiar pain stabbed in her head as she threw the covers to one side. Her mouth was pasty and dry. She felt dizzy, too, the walls cocking slightly like a funhouse room. Her eyes darted involuntarily to the rug covering the trap door to the cellar. It was down there. *Don't get crazy*, she thought. Composing herself on the edge of the bed, she rose unsteadily and worked her way to the door. There was the electric snap of fear when the door did not yield right away, and Sarah panicked, jerking it open with both hands, the jagged filament of hysteria breaking as she staggered backward from the effort. Steadying herself, she looked cautiously around the living room before walking softly to the kitchen, where she turned on the light and peered around again.

When she was convinced it was safe, she moved to the bathroom, clicked on the light and closed the door. Her ashen face stared back at her in the mirror. She tilted her head back and inspected her nose. No blood. But her tongue was coated in a thick white film that she scraped with her fingernail, then scrubbed with her toothbrush until she felt she would retch. She ran hot water in the sink, rinsing the toothbrush thoroughly. A wave of fatigue washed over her as she dropped the toothbrush in its holder and gripped the edge of the basin, her knees buckling slightly. Leaning against the counter, she rested on her elbows until the feeling subsided. From that position she could see the underside of the medicine chest, a thin layer of mould speckling its bottom. She would need more than aspirin tonight.

Rows of plastic amber prescription bottles lined the glass shelves. Sarah selected one cautiously. Valium. She checked the date, opened it, inspected the odd assortment of coloured pills inside, then replaced it and chose another, hidden at the back of the chest. It was a big bottle of codeine, nearly full. Maybe a hundred tablets or more, she estimated.

"Thanks, Mom," she said, taking several white pills from the bottle and slipping them into the breast pocket of her pyjamas before replacing the codeine carefully on the shelf. "Reserves," she said, laughing softly. She stood staring into the medicine chest, then let out a deep sigh as she decided on a wrinkled and years-old cold remedy packet.

As Sarah filled the kettle with water and placed it on the stove, she had the dark sensation of being watched. She canvassed the windows in the kitchen, checking to see if the curtains were all closed. The window on the kitchen door was exposed, the white curtain drawn to one side. Moving slowly toward the door, Sarah approached it so as not to be seen through the window and tugged the curtain across. Counting several beats to herself, she glided back to the stove where the kettle waited. But when she reached for the dial, a phantom hand brushed the hair at the back of her neck. She froze. Her skin tingled lightly. *He's toying with you, trying to set you off balance.*

"All right!" she yelled, spinning around and staring wildly across the room. She turned, snapped the dial on the stove to high, folded her arms across her chest and leaned with her back to the kettle, one hand massaging her neck. The kettle clicked and clucked behind her as the element heated to a red glow. Before the whistle had a chance to sound, Sarah pulled the kettle from the burner and turned the dial to off. The water steamed and sloshed into the mug. The foil packet was difficult to open, the powder sticking to the pouch in a big clump from the bathroom damp. Sarah worked it with her hands, breaking the clump into chunks and dropping them in the mug. Grabbing a teaspoon, she hurried back to her room, leaving a trail of lights behind her.

Before closing the bedroom door, she tested the handle to

make sure it wouldn't stick again, then she slipped into bed, covering her legs with layers of blankets. As she stirred the medicine, the bright *ting, ting, ting* of the teaspoon against the sides of the mug sounded somehow eerie in the quiet of her room. She took a tentative sip. It was a familiar taste, sweet and slightly acidic. It was the same medicine she used to drink at night in the hospital to calm her mind. Near the end when she had started keeping a twenty-four-hour vigil, she'd depended on it. It was all she could do to cope with the erratic rhythms of the hospital.

The nurses worked in twelve-hour shifts. Four days on, three days off. It made things difficult. In the somnambulant world of chronic care, change was disruptive. A new set of eyes and hands. The endless questions. How much of this? How much of that? Legs covered? Legs exposed? No oral medication. Intravenous only. The high-pitched efficiency of staff recharged from the weekend, the counterfeit friendliness ground to an inert powder by the end of the week. The patients didn't like change. They didn't like getting used to new personalities. "Watch out for that one," one of them told her. "She's a witch." And always the concern that the nurse would wilfully screw up, administer the wrong dose or wrong medicine entirely, indifferent face cocked to one side, neat white shoes touching, manicured hands patiently clasped.

By the time she finished the medicine, Sarah could feel it beginning to work, her eyes heavy and drooping, her fear deadened. Placing the empty mug on the crate beside her bed, she settled in. But the light—should she sleep with it on? She couldn't bear the idea of the dark right now. She lay for a moment thinking about what she should do, then rolled over and faced the wall, covering her head with the blankets.

✻　✻　✻

"I think I saw John," Sarah announced out of the blue at the Queen's. She didn't know how else to open such a conversation.

Donna lowered her coffee cup. "What do you mean? Like a ghost?"

Sarah pushed her french fries around her plate. "Yeah, I guess so."

"Tell me all about it," Donna said, sitting up excitedly in the booth.

"There's not much to tell."

"Come on, Wagner!"

"He came into my room. He stood beside the bed. That's it."

"Holy crap, this is great!"

"Yeah, sure." Sarah sat back in her seat. *Here we go.* Donna would find a way to make a three-ring circus out of the whole thing if she wasn't careful.

"Do you know how badly I've wanted an experience like that?" Donna asked.

Sarah sighed, taking a cigarette and lighting it. "Nice for you, Donna, but I don't find it particularly thrilling. It's scary. I mean, what does he want from me? And how do I know I'm not just nuts?" She twirled the cigarette nervously on the edge of the ashtray. She should have just kept it between herself and Michael. At least he didn't ask for explanations. He seemed to simply understand how she felt without asking her to define it. It was strange how they could communicate and not have to say a word sometimes.

"Maybe he's having trouble crossing over," Donna proffered hopefully. She pushed her coffee cup away and began eating Sarah's french fries.

"What do you mean . . . like, to the other side?"

"Yeah. Maybe he's stuck in limbo or something."

Sarah picked up a fry, swirled it in the ketchup and abandoned it at the edge of the plate when a wave of nausea threatened. The ketchup looked too much like blood. "I suppose it's possible," she said.

"Of course it's possible," Donna asserted. "And it's nothing to be ashamed of. There are lots of books about it. Our culture is so tight-assed when it comes to anything even remotely connected to death. We don't recognize it as a part of life, the cycle of all living things. In Mexico they celebrate the Day of the Dead."

Sarah shook her head. "I don't think a parade is going to help matters much."

"Not a parade," Donna said. "Something more intimate, more personal. Some kind of ritual."

A ritual, Sarah thought. *Is that what John needs?*

"Some people just don't want to let go," Donna continued. "They are so deeply entrenched in this corporeal plane that they can't imagine anything else. So they hang around, occupy the same spaces they did in life, go through the same routines. They become ghosts . . . And most of them don't even know they're dead." She whispered this last part like it was a national secret.

Sarah considered the notion. "He loved living," she agreed.

"Of course he did," Donna jumped in, apparently happy that her words had hit home. She tossed the fry she'd been toying with onto the plate and brushed her hands together. "Come on. Let's go to the bookstore."

* * *

There were two whole walls of titles in the Witchcraft section, everything from dream analysis to spell and charm books. "I don't know," Sarah murmured, browsing the shelves.

"Listen to this," Donna said. She opened a blue hardcover called *The Hidden Meaning of Things* and began to read. "'Psychologically, the forest is often interpreted as a symbol of the unconscious, where there are secrets to be discovered and perhaps dark emotions and memories to be faced.'"

"Hmmm. Interesting," Sarah said without conviction. She continued to peruse the titles.

"There's more. 'Forests were considered places of mystery and transformation, and were therefore the rightful home to sorcerers and enchanters. The tree was believed to be infused with both divine and creative energy by the ancients.'"

The tree. The oak from Sarah's dreams appeared in her mind, its leaves shining enigmatically in the dark. From somewhere deep in the woods, the girl beckoned. "No," Sarah said, dismissing the image. "I need something specifically about ghosts."

Donna sighed, shut the book and replaced it on the shelf. "Okay, here's one . . . *Rituals for Everyday Life.*"

THE BOOK OF LIVING anD DYING

Sarah glanced at the yellow cover and shook her head.

Donna discarded it, yanking another from the shelf. "What about this? *The Book of Living and Dying.*" She held the book up. It had a faded black leather cover with white letters, shaped like little bones.

"It looks used," Sarah said, taking the book. It had a slightly musty smell. She opened it to the first page. The type was heavy and old fashioned, the paper filmy and yellowed. Parchment of some sort. Below the title, there was a pen-and-ink drawing of a spiral floating in an ocean of stars. Leafing quickly through the pages, Sarah landed on a section entitled "Ghosts." She read a few sentences, then closed the book excitedly. "This one seems good."

"Excellent!" Donna said. She rose from the floor, where she had been sitting cross-legged, and brushed herself off. "We can get started right away."

Sarah didn't answer but walked up to the counter and placed the book face down in front of the sales clerk. The woman promptly flipped it over and read the title out loud. She searched unsuccessfully for the price, then checked the computer. When nothing came up, she held the book in the air and called loudly for the manager.

"Have you seen *The Tibetan Book of the Dead*?" she chattered as they waited.

Sarah glanced nervously over her shoulder at the man standing behind her in line. "No, I haven't," she said.

"It's a *wonderful* text," the clerk continued. "I think everyone should read it."

The manager finally appeared, a teenager, apparently, in a vest too big for his thin chest. He inspected the book and scratched his head. "Must be old stock," he said, entering a code into the computer.

The total came to nine dollars and ninety-nine cents. Before the clerk could bag the book, Sarah grabbed it from the counter and stuffed it into her knapsack. Punching her PIN number into the keypad, she waited for the approval prompt to light up the screen as the clerk stood, bank card held casually in the air. Once the machine began to ring the transaction through, the clerk handed the card back to Sarah.

"Have a great day," she called out cheerfully as Sarah and Donna left the store.

"We can do it at my house," Donna offered. "I've always wanted to do something like this. You know I've been into this kind of stuff for a while, but I've never had the opportunity to do it for real, for something serious like this."

"You mean, like *The Exorcist*?" Sarah said. She placed her hand on her friend's arm. "I appreciate everything you've done, Donna. But I think I need to do this alone."

Donna's face crumpled in disappointment. "But it helps if you have more than one person. It creates more positive energy . . ." She saw the refusal in Sarah's face and relented. "Fine, Wagner. Whatever. It's your ghost."

"Thanks," Sarah said. "I'll tell you how it goes, I promise."

✳   ✳   ✳

It was rare to find her mother away from home. Sarah checked the rooms twice, to make sure. But it was true. She was alone. She threw her jacket over the back of the couch, opened her knapsack and pulled the book out. Kicking off her shoes, she curled like a cat in one corner of the sofa and turned eagerly to the section on ghosts. She discovered almost immediately that hauntings are rarely violent or indiscriminate. More often they are personal, generated by the incapacity of the living to atone for the loss of the dead. Hadn't Michael said something similar? Sarah felt a sudden rush of gratitude. Here was the answer before her, and the knowledge that she was not alone. She wasn't crazy. The book was proof of that. Other people had had the same experience. She checked the cover for the author's name but couldn't find one. She searched the pages inside. Nothing. "How odd."

Turning back to the chapter, Sarah learned that death can be confusing for the dead. That sometimes they get lost in their journey to the other side. It seemed that it was up to the living to help the spirit of the deceased, to let it know what has happened. She paused, considering this. Had John's spirit simply got lost? At the bottom of the passage, a ritual was described. It began with a series of items. Sarah made a list of the things she would need: an altar appropriately set up (she put a question mark after this), a photo of the dead person, tea-lights, sheets of paper and pencils, an apple, a pin, a cauldron and, if possible, a statue of the Lady or Lord—whoever they were.

Sarah dog-eared the page in the book and looked at her list. She didn't have a cauldron or statue of the Lady or Lord. She did have a small jade Buddha, though, and a heavy glass ashtray—there were lots of ashtrays in the house. Would these substitutions affect the magic? There was no way to know for sure. She rose to collect the necessary items and found herself drawn to her mother's room. When was the last time she'd been in there?

Stepping cautiously inside, Sarah looked around the room, at its austerity. The single bed, neat as a matchbox.

The walls, white, unadorned. A pine night table next to the bed. White curtains on the window. A small veneered dresser with round wooden knobs. A metal rod behind the door displaying a handful of dowdy dresses. No wonder her mother had no will, she thought. She'd divested herself of earthly trappings, like she was expecting to die any minute.

Beneath the bed was a cardboard box with a lid, as though the bed had laid an egg in its own image. Sarah reached in and pulled the box out. It was filled with papers and old cards. Picking up a card from the top, she read the inscription: "To a Dear Mother." On the inside, beneath a gold-lettered poem, was John's handwriting. *"Have a good one, Mum!"* There were cards for Christmas, Easter, Mother's Day—all from John. The dutiful son. There were letters, too, and short notes. *I'll try to make it for Thanksgiving. Save some bird for me. John.* Interspersed among the cards were receipts for things: some cans of paint, a pair of shoes, a book. And then a larger receipt, folded. Sarah opened it and looked at the letterhead at the top. "Fine Funerals." She read the description, the details in meticulous handwritten script. *"Basic Funeral Package: Blue Horizons, pine with brass accents. Cremation and burial service. Newspaper announcement—free."* The whole thing, with announcement gratuity, had set her mother back $3,500. Sarah folded the receipt and placed it to one side of the box.

She picked up a postcard: *The Three Fates.* The picture on the front showed an etching of three women sitting side by side, holding a skein of wool. The woman in the middle held shears poised, ready to cut the yarn. There was something eerily calculating about the women, with their dispassionate faces. On the back of the card was a quotation, written in pencil: *"Who knows but life be that which men call death, and death what men call life?"* The handwriting unfamiliar. What was this doing in her mother's things? It seemed out of place among the Christmas cards and scraps of old paper. Sarah set the postcard aside, thinking it was somehow appropriate for the ritual, even though it wasn't on the list.

Digging through the papers, Sarah began looking for something—anything—with her name on it. Hadn't she given her mother cards over the years? When she reached the bottom of the box, she felt oddly disappointed. Why had her mother kept letters from John but not from her? There was no denying that they didn't get along. But to be so final, so dismissive . . . Sarah found it upsetting. It was as if she were being slowly erased. "What do you expect?" she muttered, piling the papers back in the box, careful to place the cards she had found first at the top. She didn't want her mother to know she had been snooping.

Sliding the box to its spot under the bed, Sarah picked up the postcard of the three women and moved into the kitchen to collect the rest of the things she would need. But as she reached to open a drawer, a wave of dizziness set her back on her heels. *He's doing this to me,* she thought, grasping the counter in alarm, then remembering that she had only had coffee with Donna earlier. Coffee and Advil. She would eat after the ritual, she promised herself as the dizzy spell passed.

The pin was easy to find, but there were no tea-lights in the kitchen. There were several half-burned white tapers, though, and a box of matches. In place of a candlestick an empty green wine bottle from under the sink would have to do. Sarah pushed the snub end of a taper into the wine bottle, the wax curling over the lip like a strip of old cheese. The apple she found in the fridge, its skin slightly puckered. She checked her list: "An altar appropriately set up." What that meant she wasn't sure, but she felt it must involve a white cloth of some kind; a white towel from the bathroom was all she had.

Placing the altar trappings on her bed, Sarah cleared the milk crate, moved it to the centre of the room and covered it with the towel. The towel was too long, so she tucked it under at the sides, smoothing it with her hands. She set the wine bottle, pin and apple in the middle of the crate, took the jade Buddha from the top of her dresser, wiped it clean with her shirt and placed it next to the wine bottle. Retrieving her box of photos from the dresser, she chose a picture of John that wasn't one of her favourites but clearly showed his features and his guitar. Leaning the photo against the wine bottle next to the card of the three women, she returned the box to the drawer.

To set the mood, Sarah drew the curtains on her bedroom window and sat cross-legged in front of the altar, book resting in her lap. But the effect of the whole thing was somewhat discouraging. With the wine bottle candle and the white towel, the altar looked like a prop table setting at a French restaurant in a high school play. It lacked authenticity, she thought, even though she had no idea what an altar was supposed to look like. It needed . . . something. Scouring her room, Sarah chose a handful of leaves, a small mesh bundle of shells she had purchased as a young girl and a tiny wooden basket the size of a walnut. Inside the basket, on a bed of cotton, a gold-and-green beetle gleamed, salvaged from the sidewalk years earlier. Rearranging the altar, Sarah placed the leaves and shells with the beetle beside the apple and was finally satisfied with the way things looked.

"'Light the candle,'" she read in a hushed voice. She took

the box of matches, drew one from the carton and lit it. The candle guttered in the draft from the bedroom window, a clear teardrop of wax rolling down one side and spilling onto the green glass of the wine bottle before congealing and hardening into a translucent exclamation mark. Sarah reached over and extinguished the bedroom light with a snap; the candle bathed the room with its glow.

"'Cleanse the pin in the fire and prick the deceased's name in the skin of the apple, promising to resolve the conflict in your heart. Eat the apple and bury the core in the earth.'"

The pin made tiny puncture sounds as it pierced the skin. When she was finished writing John's name, Sarah started to eat. The apple tasted dry and slightly sour. She couldn't finish the whole thing but made sure to eat the parts with his name, placing the rest on the altar beside the candle. She closed her eyes, the way the book said, and thought about John. How did seeing him make her feel? She sat in silence for several minutes, allowing images to flicker through her mind. She wasn't sure, really, how to summarize the way she felt. John's ghost beside the bed; his face reflected in the bathroom mirror; the constant, unsettling feeling of being watched . . . Was that what the book meant? Sarah opened her eyes and peered at the page in the candlelight:

"What message do you wish to convey to your loved one?"

Her mind was as blank as the piece of paper in front of her. She could think of nothing except her own fear at seeing him and the niggling guilt over her errant thoughts when he was sick. The candle flame sputtered. A shiver ran like a millipede up the ladder of her spine. What message would he want to hear? she wondered. What would make him forgive her?

I love you, a voice in her head said.

"*I love you,*" she wrote in heavy letters on the page, then added several Xs and Os as an afterthought.

She folded the paper in quarters around the photo, the way the book had said to do, creasing the edges neatly with her thumbs. Holding one corner of the bundle to the candle, she watched as the fire leapt to consume her message, the paper curling and blackening quickly, the photo burning more slowly, blue and green flames moving over John's face like phosphorescent liquid, blistering his eyes, his smile, his hair. She held the photo, the smoke rising to the ceiling of her room, until the flames threatened to singe her fingers, then dropped the bundle into the glass ashtray, the fire ebbing as the photo withered into a small pile of delicate ash.

"Recite a prayer," the book said. There were so many to choose from. Sarah finally decided on one called "Releasing the Spirit."

> Earth, relinquish this soul
> Wind, carry this soul
> Sky embrace this soul
> No longer of this world
> Free of pain
> Of mortal concerns
> Take flight
> The wings of love shall carry you
> Set you free
> So mote it be

The weight of silence bore heavily upon her as she spoke the final words of the prayer. Was that all it took to relieve the dead? It didn't seem like enough. She looked at the altar. The postcard of the three women stared back at her. Picking up the card, she held it to the flame. It resisted burning, but the cold faces of the women succumbed at last to the heat. *A spoonful of your own medicine,* Sarah thought, dropping the card into the ashtray and watching as the women were reduced to cinders next to the remains of John's photo. Feeling she should do more still, she leafed through the book again, stopping at a page marked "The Wisdom of the Dead." "The living," the book instructed, "can benefit by divesting themselves of earthly trappings such as clothes to experience the true freedom of surrender."

Removing her clothes for the sake of ritual seemed strange at first, but by the time Sarah was completely naked she had to admit that she felt surprisingly light. She laughed as she licked her thumb and finger to snuff the candle before tucking herself beneath the blankets. Lying in bed, the sheets felt cool and comfortable against her bare skin and she found herself feeling somewhat relieved, even hopeful. If the ritual worked, she would be free of John's ghost—and maybe even her own guilt. She began to think about him, about the months he'd spent in bed. His hopelessness. The fire of life guttering inside him. Waiting for the end to come. Not with a bang, but with a whimper. It wasn't the big things that got you in the end, she knew, it was the little things, innocuous little bugs and invisible viruses that normal people could easily fend off.

"A cold can be fatal to a chronic care patient," the nurse carefully explained. "The immune system, already ravaged by disease, can't muster the forces to battle a simple virus. Most of the patients that enter the chronic care ward die from pneumonia or some other unrelated illness," she added. And perhaps it was better that way. Better than waiting for the

unconditional surrender of a heart that didn't know enough to stop beating. The body, long since decayed by disease, could give up weeks—sometimes months—before the heart stuttered to a halt.

The announcement that the nurses had detected fever made her delirious with worry, and then, surprisingly, shamefully, hopeful. If there was the chance to slip quietly into unconsciousness, to die peacefully while asleep, wouldn't it be better for all of them? But it was unbearable to think about, now that it was a distinct possibility. Rounding the corner to find the empty bed newly made, the floors scrubbed, curtains drawn to let the sunlight in.

In the morning it was business as usual, though, the irritation and anger rising before the nurse arrived with the morning meds. The fever descending slowly throughout the day, stabilizing by dinner. The priest showed up all the same, sparking terror throughout the ward, gliding silently down the hall in his black frock, a benign expression described artfully on his face. Sitting in a chair beside the bed, he didn't talk at all about death or dying, or even God, but spoke instead about horses and Ireland.

CHAPTER seven

The ritual didn't work. Sarah knew that when she woke and found John sitting on the edge of her bed. He was hunched over, face in his hands. She would have screamed right away if she hadn't glanced at his feet. He was wearing blue dress socks, no shoes. Wasn't that how it had been in the end? His feet, too swollen with illness for anything but socks or a pair of knit slippers. There was something innocent and sad about his sock feet, as though he wasn't quite ready for the trip he was supposed to make. *Haven't you got your shoes on yet?*

Sarah closed her eyes and counted to ten. She must have done something wrong. Instead of freeing his spirit from its earthly chains she had invited it back. He began calling her name, his voice thick and distorted, like he was speaking with a throat full of milk.

"No!" Sarah shrieked, covering her ears with her hands. When she opened her eyes again, he was gone, the end of the bed empty, the room oppressively silent. She burst into tears of hopelessness and frustration and rage. What recourse did she have now? A flash of hatred seared her heart. Why wouldn't he just go away and leave her alone? And then her mind flipped instantly over. This was Donna's fault. Her and her stupid ideas.

Picking up the book from the altar, Sarah hurled it at the bedroom door. It missed its mark, hitting the wall with a loud clunk and flapping like a gun-shot partridge to the foot of her dresser. She yanked one corner of the towel, crashing the contents of the altar to the floor, the ashes spilling over the apple as it tumbled. *The apple*. She was supposed to have buried it. She kicked the milk crate to one side, got dressed and stormed from the room, leaving the mess behind. She was going to Michael's. She would stay with him.

✻   ✻   ✻

Michael slept, his hair an ebony river across the white fabric of the pillow, the gentle rhythm of his breathing as soothing as a cat's purr. Sarah felt safe beside him. She didn't mind that he slept while she lay awake. He hadn't questioned her when she'd arrived, tapping on his bedroom window. He'd simply helped her through and then held her, kissing her eyes and mouth as he worked her clothes off and eased her into bed next to him. They'd slept, holding each other, until Sarah had startled awake. She'd looked around the room, frantically, before realizing where she was and settling back in again.

Inching herself free from his embrace, she rolled onto her side and casually inspected the contents of the cubby beside his bed. Her eyes rested on a small plastic bag. Dehydrated stems of some sort—maybe mushrooms. She held the bag to her nose and sniffed. She'd never done mushrooms before but knew people who had. It was an outdated high, a hippie drug. She wondered what it would be like to be stoned on mushrooms, to really let go and hallucinate. She'd always been afraid to lose control—she'd seen it happen to other people. Mushrooms were strong medicine, she'd heard. Maybe as strong as morphine.

Morphine was for terminally ill patients only. The doctor had been quite clear about that. There were concerns about addiction and substance abuse. The hospital had rules.

The doctor was a hard sell. It took arguments—several of them and quite heated—before he relented and signed the release form. Moments later a haughty young nurse strode into the room, syringe in hand. She jerked the gown sleeve clear up to the shoulder, swiped the elbow joint with an alcohol-soaked cotton ball and stabbed the needle in, depressing the plunger with unnecessary force, the morphine shooting in, until it seemed as though the vein would burst. She left without a word, leaving the gown sleeve still pushed up and crumpled at the shoulder.

Michael rolled over and spooned up behind her. "You found my stash," he said, nuzzling her ear.

"I want to try it."

"You've never done it before?"

Sarah lay silent.

"Okay, babe," he conceded, pushing her hair aside and kissing the back of her neck. "But I have rules."

✳   ✳   ✳

Michael moved easily through the forest, a leather bag on his shoulder. He helped Sarah along, holding branches for her, guiding her over stumps and around rocks. They walked through the cedars, the sweet green branches scenting the air with the fragrance of pepper and lemon. The night enveloped them, the moon hiding shyly behind a veil of clouds. At a small clearing encircled with stones they stopped, the cedars creating an arbour above them. "Sit here," he said, moving her toward a boulder that shone like a bone in the dark.

He sat on a rock across from her, bag at his feet. "Do you believe in the spirit world?"

Sarah stared silently back at him. She didn't know what she believed any more.

"Tonight, you will know for certain," Michael continued, working the leather bag open. Pulling out four small candles, he placed them at four corners within the circle of stones. He walked in a clockwise direction, pointing his hand in front of himself, then lit the candles, one by one, the faint smell of sulphur hanging in the air as the candle flames winked against the darkness. "I call upon the four elements for protection," he said, reaching into the bag and pulling out a small pouch also made of leather. He loosened the tie from the top of the bag and began sprinkling some kind of herb before the candles. "Tobacco," he said, answering her unspoken question. "An offering." He returned to his stone and pulled a length of white rope from the bag, fixing her with a stern stare. "You must be cleansed before your journey. What sexual encounters have you engaged in?" He held the rope out in his hands.

Sarah giggled. Michael remained expressionless.

"Ummm . . . real, or imagined?" Sarah asked, trying to match his mood.

"Real."

"I've had . . . relations with a half-breed," she said, smiling.

Michael did not respond, but tied a knot in the rope and then looked at her expectantly.

"I slept with Cole Olsen in eleventh grade because I had a dream that he was really good in bed," Sarah said.

Michael tied another knot.

"He wasn't," she added. "I lost my virginity to our family physician. We did it on the examination table."

Another knot.

"I'm just kidding about that." Laughing nervously, she cleared her throat, then composed herself and continued. "I lost my virginity to my tenth grade boyfriend . . ." She hesitated, wondering if she should tell the truth. "It was Peter. Peter Burrows."

She thought she saw something glimmer in his eyes, something he was trying to suppress. Jealousy, maybe? If it was, he controlled it well. He tied several knots in the rope.

"That's it. Not very exciting, is it?"

Michael didn't answer but walked over to one of the candles and held the rope over the flame. The fire tongued greedily at the rope, the fibres curling and burning orange as the flames skipped hungrily up. Michael dropped the rope to the ground in the centre of the circle, where it continued to burn like a snake doused in kerosene. He spoke in an otherworldly voice. "Fire has cleansed you, unhinged your spirit from this mortal coil." Sitting down on the rock, he produced another small leather pouch and untied it. He pulled out the dried mushroom stalks and handed her a small portion. "Swallow these."

Sarah put the mushrooms in her mouth, half chewed them and swallowed. They tasted dusty, earthy. Michael did the same but took more than her, she noticed. Wrapping the leather cord carefully around the top of the pouch, he retied it adeptly and pushed it into his breast pocket. He stood up and pulled her to her feet. "Come on."

They wove through the trees, the wind picking up, rustling the cedars. Sarah broke off a small branch. Crushing it in her fingers, she released the lemony scent and rubbed it under her nose. "Wait," she called out to Michael, who had run ahead. "I have something for you." She thought she saw him stop next to a stand of birch trees in the distance, but he was next to her, gripping her arm.

"Listen," he said.

She strained to hear. A twig snapped somewhere deep in the woods. There was a soft murmuring. Michael stepped forward and a huge buck exploded from behind a thicket, leaping through the air, white tail flashing. Sarah was sure she saw sparks fly as the deer's feet touched the ground, a silver trail tracing its path as it fled through the woods. Michael bolted after it, eyes wild, hair streaming.

"Wait for me," Sarah called. She ran after him, stumbling through the underbrush, tripping over roots. Her legs felt weak, her head spinning. "Wait!" She stopped to catch her breath, the sound of her own breathing so loud she had to put her hands over her ears to stop it. She looked around for Michael. He had left her alone. *Why would he do that?* As she searched through the forest she began seeing John's face everywhere, in the leaves, in the stones on the ground, in the sky. He was coming to get her. At the brink of panic, she forced herself to count trees, speaking their names. *"Quercus rubra. Quercus alba. Ostrya virginiana. Betula papyrifera."*

At the birch trees she stopped. Their smooth white bark glowed like abalone in the moonlight. She suddenly saw

Michael ahead of her, crouching behind some bushes. She moved toward him and hunched over. He grabbed her shirt, pulled her down and pointed at something in the clearing ahead. It was a couple writhing together on the ground, the woman moaning. The deer stood over them, poised, motionless. Sarah could almost see the woman's face, the man's back glistening in the dark, his feet capped with socks. *How strange.* Just like the time she'd seen her parents making love, the shame of it. Tramping into their room to find her father on top of her mother, her mother's face oddly vacant, her father naked except for the blue socks pulled halfway up his calves. The fleeting glimpse of them punctuating his bare legs, the rest of his body exposed, like a clothing store mannequin, before her mother cried out and her father sprang angrily from the bed.

Sarah turned to look at Michael but he was gone. The couple was gone too. Only the deer remained, majestic against a backdrop of stars that pulsated with energy, the moon's face appearing stark and startled above the tree branches as the clouds lifted. The buck met her gaze, then disappeared without a sound into the trees, and Sarah was immediately overcome with a feeling of great loneliness. Why had everyone forsaken her? Why must she always be alone? Abject sorrow swept over her and would have taken her under if she hadn't seen the figure step out from behind a large oak tree. It shimmered in the most seductive way, like sunlight under water. Somehow Sarah knew that it was a girl—*the girl.* At once she could see impossible detail, the green cotton thread of the girl's dress, the shadows of her knees against the fabric. But the face . . . she could not see the face. The girl beckoned to Sarah, urging her to come closer. Sarah's heart beat loudly in her chest and then the whole forest seemed to be beating in sympathy with her heart. She moved toward the girl as in a trance, the pull irresistible, as if she was being drawn by some unseen hand to this image she had known only in photographs. All her teenage musings, all her childish fears would be quelled if only she could reach the girl.

As she stepped forward, she heard another twig snap, thought it must be the deer, then felt a hand grasp her ankle. Michael lay on the ground, stripped to the waist, the lower half of his face now painted black. He had an apple in his hand. He held it up to her.

"Take your clothes off," he said.

* * *

Sarah woke to the sound of the phone ringing. She sat up on one elbow—the pain erupting in her skull—and flopped back down on the bed. The phone rang and rang. Why didn't her mother answer it? Trying to muffle the sound, she pressed a pillow over her head. It had to be Donna, calling to find out where she was. She would call and call and call. Sarah lay with her head under her pillow, the silence ringing in the brief pauses between telephone sieges, until at last she couldn't stand it any longer and threw the pillow to one side. Kicking the covers off her legs, she discovered that she was still in her clothes. Had she gone out at all, or simply fallen asleep fully dressed? Sitting with her head in her hands, she struggled to remember her night with Michael. The deer, the couple writhing—*and the girl*. Hadn't she seen the girl from the photos? She moaned lightly. How had

Michael described it? "A hallucinatory projection stimu-lated by chemicals and fabricated in the darker recesses of her imagination." The mushrooms had certainly worked their magic.

Sarah pulled her hands from her face and was shocked to find them smeared with black paint. Standing up to look in the vanity mirror she saw her face painted in the image of a skull. He must have done that. She bared her teeth at the mirror; they looked surprisingly white. The phone began to ring again. "Get lost," she said as she searched her desk for cream and some tissues and proceeded to remove the paint. It resisted at first but slid off easily once the cream was worked in. After dropping the dirty tissues in wet clumps into the wastebasket, Sarah cleaned her hands as well, dry-ing her palms on the legs of her jeans.

The phone continued to ring. She heard her mother get up at last, heard the bedroom door creak open, footsteps scuffling across the living room to the kitchen. The phone stopped mid ring and there was silence. Sarah listened. Her mother rattled around the kitchen, tap water running, the sound of the coffee maker gurgling. She must have discon-nected the phone.

Retrieving her pyjama top from the floor, Sarah checked the pocket for the codeine tablets. She found the pills, pushed them into her mouth and swallowed. They stuck in the back of her throat. Not as easy to take as aspirin. Because she didn't want to risk bumping into her mother in the kitchen to get a glass of water, she swallowed repeatedly, like a frog, until the pills dislodged from her throat, only to lodge a short way down her windpipe. She coughed, her eyes watering, the pressure in her head rising with the effort as she fought to catch her breath. A fleeting image of John asserted itself along with the suddenly remembered failed ritual. The ash-covered and half-eaten apple still lay on the floor, next to the wine bottle and the gold-and-green beetle. She'd forgotten to bury it. She would do that today. Bury it in the earth, the way the book had told her to do in the first place. She had another idea, too, one she'd gleaned from Michael.

Once the codeine pills had dissolved, Sarah grabbed her binders of photos and flipped to the back, where she kept the pictures of John's gigs. Dozens of snapshots, some black and white, some colour. John holding the Fender. John singing, the guitar hanging across his hips from its strap. John on stage in Germany. In Chicago. In Toronto. She'd studied the pictures so many times, she knew every line on his face, every expression. Peeling back the acetate, Sarah carefully pried the photos from their pages, stacking them neatly on the bed beside her. She chose several from each time frame. When she was finished, she took an envelope, placed the photos inside and folded it shut, securing it with a paper clip from her desk. Slipping the packet into the side pocket of her knapsack, she included a copy of John's CD—his only CD— then zipped the pocket shut. Her calculus book peeked out the top of her knapsack. "Oh, no," she groaned, remembering the test she had to study for. She considered going back to bed but vetoed the idea and decided to take a shower instead to wake herself up.

Her mother was sitting at the kitchen table, her face as grey as ashes. "Bloody phone," she muttered.

Sarah walked silently past, closing the door to the bathroom before tearing the shower curtain to one side, checking, then searching the cupboard under the sink. She even snapped a towel loudly, convinced the noise would scare away any marauding spirits. When the steam from the tub filled the bathroom, she wiped the mirror quickly with her hand, just in case John got any ideas. She did it again when she got out of the shower, but found only her own face staring back at her.

＊　＊　＊

Sarah sat in bed with her calculus book on her lap, a glass of water on the milk crate beside her. She'd buried the apple core beneath the locust tree in the yard, once her mother had vacated the kitchen. The dirt still clung stubbornly beneath her fingernails even though she'd washed her hands several times. The rest of the altar she'd simply tossed into a box in her closet, using the towel to wipe the ashes from the floor. Now she was resting in bed, her hands on the pages of her math text. The codeine was taking effect, burnishing the edge off the ragged pain in her head. Rising from the page, the words and numbers began to shift and roll like beach pebbles lapped by water. A tiny red spider appeared at the edge of the book and navigated slowly through the floating letters, across the top of the page and down the spine, disappearing into the cleft. As her head lolled heavily back, the book slipped from Sarah's hands to one side of the bed.

She was in the forest, the trees breathing all around her, the cries of the woman resonating deep within the soil. She was following the girl, her form a light shape in the distance along the path. They were moving toward the oak tree, its branches slowly swaying. Sarah looked down and saw that her feet were bare. The rest of her was naked too, her breasts shining like the palest of opals, her skin smooth and glimmering, interrupted only by the dark mound between her legs. She did not feel shame but was amazed at how her feet seemed to skim the ground effortlessly, without breaking a single branch. As she ran, she moved closer and closer to the girl, the girl's back now a sharp outline against the dusky light of the forest. Reaching out to touch her, Sarah's fingers barely brushed the cool fabric of the girl's dress when a hand slipped into her own. It was John's hand. Glaring at her, he opened his mouth to speak but emitted a high-pitched shriek instead. The shrieking grew louder and louder as Sarah struggled to pull away from him, until she was forced, sputtering and gasping like a drowning swimmer, to the surface of her dream. It was the phone again. Reaching to turn on the light, she knocked the glass of water from the milk crate and sent it splashing to the floor.

❊　❊　❊

A man 1.8 metres tall approaches a lamppost at 1.6 metres per second. If the lamp is hanging 6 metres above the ground, at what speed is the length of his shadow changing when he is 3 metres from the lamp?

Sarah stared at the question on the page. It made her head hurt just to look at it. Why was the man out walking at night in the first place? Next question.

A stone is dropped into a lake, creating a circular ripple that travels outward at a speed of 25 centimetres per second. Find the rate at which the area within the circle is increasing after 4 seconds.

What would happen if she just got up and left? Sarah wondered. She tapped her pencil absently against her lips, chewing her gum. She looked over at Donna's empty seat, then at Michael. He was smiling at her, tapping his pencil against his lips in synchrony with hers.

A stone is dropped into a lake, creating a circular ripple that engenders an entire universe to pour from the water at a speed of 25 light years per second . . .

"Okay, people," Mr. Kovski announced. "Stop writing. Pass your papers to the front, please."

Sarah slashed a pencil stroke across the test paper. She erased her name at the top of the page, crumpled the paper into a ball and handed it to "Beth the Brain," the girl Donna nicknamed Rubik's Cube. Beth blinked at the wad of paper through her thick glasses, then back at Sarah, sympathetically.

Sarah shrugged. "It doesn't matter."

Beth nodded, handed the papers forward, the ball carefully balanced on top of the other tests. Pushing away from her desk, Sarah swung her knapsack over her shoulder and made her way out of the class. Michael was waiting for her in the hall.

"How'd you do?"

"Donna skipped," she said. The codeine made her voice sound disconnected and funny.

"Yeah, I noticed."

They moved through the hallway to her locker, the bodies of the other students bumping slowly past as if they were moving through congealing gelatin.

"I have a proposition for you . . ." Sarah spoke to Michael through the gelatin.

"I like the sound of that. The answer's yes."

She leaned heavily against her locker. "You don't even know what I'm going to ask you."

"I don't need to know." He leaned next to her, watched as she turned and worked the dial on her combination lock.

"It's a project that I'm hoping you'll help me with . . . a computer thing."

"Ahh . . . a computer thing . . ."

"I'm serious."

"Yeah, yeah, of course, you know I'll help you. Why don't you come home with me?"

She couldn't help but smile. "Can I can show you later? I have band practice right now." She yanked the locker open, the familiar sound low and distant. Her reflection in the pink plastic mirror caught her up short. The circles had taken up permanent residence under her eyes. She gave her cheeks a good pinch, hoping Michael wouldn't notice how pale she looked. Pulling out the guitar, she shoved her books carelessly onto the shelf. It wasn't so neat any more.

Michael straightened himself like he was about to tell her something and was sent crashing back into the lockers. They looked up to see Peter, walking quickly away down the hall.

Prick. Sarah looked at Michael guiltily. She felt responsible for what had happened. She experienced a rush of remorse for her behaviour that instantly translated into hatred for Peter. "Don't worry, he's spineless," she said. "He won't push the issue on his own. Just hope you don't bump into him and his friends some night in a dark alley."

Michael's glare followed Peter down the hall, his face set and hard. "He'd better hope he doesn't bump into me."

❊   ❊   ❊

Peter was waiting in the music room when Sarah arrived. He was sitting in one of the hard wooden school chairs, his legs splayed out, his head cocked to one side like a belligerent husband waiting for his wife to come home. Sarah looked around the room. They were alone. Placing the guitar on a table, she dropped her bag on one of the chairs. She tried to pretend that everything was normal as she reached for the clasps on the case.

"Soooo . . ." Peter started, his voice dripping with incrimination. "You and Mortimer are quite the little item . . ."

The clasps popped, the electricity mounting in the room. Sarah felt the buzz at the back of her neck as she waited for the lightning to find its mark.

"What were you thinking, running off with half-breed trash like that?" he continued. "He'll only bring you down, Sarah. You know it."

Sarah stood over the guitar, seething, until the rage arced, blistering her brain. When she finally did look up, it wasn't so much to address him as to complete the circuit for full effect. "Who the *hell* do you think you are?" she heard herself say, the words delivered with the unnerving calm of a knife-thrower.

He stared back at her but could not hide his surprise, his feeling of betrayal. His mouth gaped open.

"Don't you ever speak to me again, do you hear me?" she continued. "Don't you ever talk to me, or look at me, don't even think about me, because you know what, Peter?" She waited, letting the edge on her words cut him to the bone. "I never loved you."

He sat up as though stabbed, his face contorting from shock to anger to pride. Sarah snapped the clasps shut and dragged the guitar case off the table. Refusing to look at him, she picked up her bag and walked from the room.

"Slut," he said as she closed the door with a click.

It wasn't until she was blocks from the school that she released a scream of frustration. She knew one thing for sure: Peter wouldn't bother her again. She would have to quit band, though. Donna would be glad of that. Or maybe not. How would Donna react to the whole thing? She could see it already, Peter spitting out his side of the story over coffee at the Queen's. And Donna would be all ears, jumping right in, she hated Michael so much. With friends like that . . .

The guitar seemed heavier than usual as she laboured along the sidewalk, the dwindling codeine no match for the familiar pain knocking furiously in her head. Sarah shifted the guitar from one hand to the other every few feet to distribute the weight. By the bridge she stopped, leaning against the stone wall for a moment so she could catch her breath before crossing to the other side. From where she was standing, she could see her secret place. She hadn't gone there in a while. She hadn't wanted to, preferring to spend her time with Michael. Just thinking of him gave her instant relief, the pressure of the day lifting as the weight of a bad dream lifts with the rising sun. She wanted to see Michael; she wanted to hear his voice. He made her feel happy. As she toiled along the dirt path up the hill to his house, she even entertained the notion of running away with him, and found herself smiling despite the pain.

When she reached the window to his bedroom she placed the guitar on the ground. Balancing on the rock, she tapped lightly on the glass. Waited for a moment, tapped again. At last his face appeared. Noticing the guitar, he motioned for her to go around to the front.

"Hey," he said as he swung the door open.

Sarah stood diffidently in the doorway. He stood too, gauging her mood, sensing that something had happened.

"I need a drink," she said.

He put his hand over hers and took the guitar, placing it against the wall. "You've come to the right place."

✻   ✻   ✻

The sound of John's guitar poured from Michael's speakers, John's image moving on the computer screen.

"Once we scan all the photos we can start to manipulate them," Michael explained. "What's this song called again?"

"'Utopian Planet.' Everyone wanted him to write lyrics for it but he refused. I love this song." Sarah sat cross-legged on a seat next to Michael, enjoying the process.

"What's 'PT Blues'?" he asked, perusing the CD liner.

"I don't know," Sarah spoke over the music. "He wouldn't tell me. He wouldn't tell anyone. I thought it was the initials of some girl that had messed with his head . . . but he would never let on. It was a secret that only he knew, and he took it to the grave."

Michael pulled the jacket from the CD case and looked through the liner notes. "Who took the pictures?"

Sarah smiled shyly. "Me. I borrowed someone's camera. I used to go to as many of his gigs as I could."

"I like them."

"We put it together in a hurry," she said with a tone of apology. "A friend of his did the cover art. Another one did the recordings. The musicians . . . they're friends of his. They donated their time for free."

"It's good," he said. "It's better than good. It's amazing. It must be hard for you to listen to it," he added softly.

The strains of John's guitar faded into the small gap of silence before the thump of the drum kit marking the beginning of the next song. "It used to be hard," she confessed. "It used to be so painful. I couldn't listen to it without crying. But it's okay now. I love to share it. I love listening to it with someone who hasn't heard it before. I'm pretty proud of him." She looked into Michael's eyes. She knew he would understand. *He's a misfit too.*

"What made you decide to do this?" he asked her.

Her mind leapt to his explanation of the near-death experience and the room filled with photos. "I thought it might help to put his spirit to rest."

"The photos you brought will work well," he said. "Almost like freeze-frame. We can take the image and animate it from one photo to the next, kind of like filling in the space between frames so it looks like he's really playing the guitar." He stared at the screen intently, mouse clicking. "It won't be as smooth as, say, a video recording, but the effect will be cool—kind of like a strobe."

"That's good ... that's great." Sarah moved closer, impressed with his knowledge. In a small act of possession, she rested her hand lightly on his shoulder. She could feel it happening, the tendrils of ownership growing between them, creeping through her consciousness, pushing deeper. He was becoming hers. She wondered if he felt it too.

"What's going on?" a voice broke in.

They both jumped, laughing guiltily. Michael's father leaned in the doorway. He wore faded jeans and a T-shirt, a white lab coat over top. Clean-shaven, hands scrubbed and neatly manicured, he was one of those men whose actual age was impossible to determine. Yet Sarah felt as though she'd seen him before, with his long salt-and-pepper hair pulled back in a thinning ponytail.

"Hi, Mr. Mort," she said, trying to sound cheerful. She gave a little wave, wondered why Michael simply turned his back and didn't introduce her. "I'm Sarah."

"Doctor," Michael's father corrected her. "It's Doctor. But just call me James." He smiled patronizingly.

"Doctor," she repeated. She felt oddly uncomfortable under his scrutiny. What was that look in his eyes? The fleeting cast she had seen in the eyes of so many men before. An appetite. Or was it something more calculating, more clinical? Disapproval? Sarah glanced at Michael but he wasn't offering any help. There was obviously some bad blood between the two, she could see that. She wasn't about to throw stones, though; she barely spoke to her own parent. Hesitating for a moment longer, Sarah finally turned her attention back to the computer monitor, her heart sinking when she caught her haggard reflection in the screen. She pushed her hair nervously behind her ears, a habit she'd had since she was a little girl. He was still standing there, she could feel it, staring at their backs. Why didn't he just go away and leave them alone?

At last he did, calling out from the kitchen. "What are you doing for dinner?"

"We already ate," Michael called back.

"The food's terrible here," he said. "I try to avoid it as much as possible."

Sarah smirked. Spoken like a true doctor. She looked out the window. It was already dark outside. Not that her mother would notice she wasn't home. But it was a long walk back. And she couldn't stay with Michael, now that his father was home.

"I should go."

"I'll walk you home," he said. He rolled the mouse, clicked, moved the image on the screen. "Just let me finish this one thing . . ."

* * *

The girl drifted through her dreams again, luring her deeper into the woods toward the tree. Sarah had almost managed to reach it when she awoke. But the dream hadn't made her feel afraid this time, she was glad to say. She felt quite cheerful, actually, lounging in bed, wearing her white flannel nightgown, the one with the buttons up the collar and long sleeves, elastic at the wrists. It felt good to wear it, even though it used to make her feel claustrophobic. Michael would laugh if he saw her bundled up like this, she thought. She didn't know why she had chosen to wear the old gown, only that she had felt somehow exposed by his father's gaze.

Her hands drifted over her flannelled body, her breasts, firm mounds beneath the fabric, her ribs a neat xylophone, the smooth hollow of her abdomen. She was definitely thinner. None of her clothes fit any more. In fact, they hung off her like bags. And with the dark circles under her eyes and her pale complexion, she had the haunted look of addiction. She blamed John for the way she looked, then quickly retracted that thought, switching her mind to Michael. She was so happy with him. But wasn't love supposed to make you glow?

There was a creak outside the bedroom door and her hands flew instantly to the covers, jerking them violently up to her chin. "Who is it?" she whispered hoarsely. She listened for several minutes, kaleidoscopic images of John's ghost spinning through her mind.

Silence. It was a false alarm.

The blankets rested heavily against her shoulder as she rolled over in bed to look at John's guitar standing in its case in the corner next to the dresser. She wondered fleetingly if it was the guitar that he wanted, then convinced herself that it was. It would explain so much. They should have cremated it down to ashes along with his body. "I'll stop playing it," she said aloud as she watched the locust tree throw dancing patterns against her bedroom wall, the tree's fingers tapping out a rhythm on the window like butterflies trapped in a jar. The codeine she had taken earlier was working its way through her veins, settling numbly at the base of her skull. It mingled with the undulating shadows in the room and began its slow, liquid dance.

She let her eyes go unfocused, the way she liked to do, and thought about John, reanimated on Michael's computer. His image captured and held within the screen, the stuttering strobe of movement, the wail of his guitar, his voice

119

crackling through the speakers from beyond the grave. From the place the disease had taken him. Dragging him by inches. Challenging the strength of the doctors' clinical faith and the power of the medical trinity: Surgery, Chemotherapy, Radiotherapy. "Brain cancer." Sarah forced herself to say the words.

A heavy shadow darkened the window, breaking the light from the street lamp and scattering the dancing branches on the wall. *It's him.* Sarah shot up in bed. She thought she heard footsteps outside her room again. There was a rattle at the door. She turned, fumbled frantically for the switch on her lamp, the cord slipping through her fingers for several moments before her thumb could find it and too late. John stood in the doorway. "Oh, please . . ." Sarah wailed, ducking under the covers, her hands shaking, the sound of her own breath like a steam engine beneath the blankets until anger overcame her and she began screaming through her fists. "Just take it!"

When she finally surfaced from the shelter of the blankets, face stained with tears, the guitar was still in its usual place in the corner.

Rising from the bed like a sleepwalker, Sarah stood in front of the mirror. Who was that girl staring back at her? She hardly recognized herself with her hair hanging dull and lifeless around her thin face. Taking the scissors from her desk, she began chopping mechanically, the scissors softly whispering as the brown locks floated to the floor. They collected at her feet, and she knew at that moment that John's ghost would never let up—ever. She would call Donna and tell her as much. Better yet, she'd tell her to her face.

CHAPTER EIGHT

Donna was being extra nice. It made Sarah suspicious. She wouldn't have thought anything of it, really, if Donna hadn't asked about Michael. In a nice way, not with the usual snide tone. She seemed really interested, *girlfriend to girlfriend*, about how things were going.

Sarah was reticent. She didn't trust Donna. And she didn't trust Peter, either. Especially since he'd shown up at the Queen's with the FEWD crowd, wearing the prescribed red-and-white-striped shirt. He hadn't acknowledged her when they'd walked in but simply pretended she wasn't there. She couldn't care less. It would make things easier, really, if he just checked himself out of her life. He hadn't spoken to her since their talk in the music room, since she'd quit band altogether. Sarah twirled her Marlboro between her fingers and looked up at Donna through the rough hem of her newly acquired bangs.

"Did you use garden shears?" Donna joked, then admitted that she liked the bangs, said they gave Sarah a sexier edge, like Angelina Jolie from *Girl, Interrupted*.

"What do you think of that?" Sarah asked, gesturing toward Peter with her cigarette.

Donna glanced over at Peter. "I guess he's been friends with them for a while. He likes to drink," she added.

Sarah shook her head, exhaling smoke in forceful disapproval. "Who am I to judge?" She said this out of formality. The truth was, she felt fully qualified to judge. She didn't like Peter one bit. He was so ordinary. She sipped her coffee, hoping Donna would swallow the platitude without question. A wave of nausea rose up to greet the pain behind her eyes and Sarah rattled her coffee cup to its saucer. "This crap tastes like motor oil," she said, grabbing her purse and digging impatiently for the pair of codeine tablets she'd put there.

Donna produced her bottle of Advil and tossed it across the table. "Keep it," she said.

Sarah's hands shook as she rattled four pills from the bottle and washed them down with a swallow of coffee.

Donna looked at her with controlled concern. "You never did tell me what was wrong with you that day."

"What day?"

Donna pointed at her nose. "The gusher."

"Oh," Sarah brushed it off with a wave. "Nothing. I'm better now," she lied. "So is my nose."

"Good," Donna said. "'cause you've been looking kind of worn out lately."

Sarah scowled. If Donna had something to say, why didn't she just come out and say it? "Of course I'm worn out," she said, her temper flaring. "That stupid ritual totally backfired. I might as well just put a 'Welcome' sign above my door."

"You saw John again?"

"Yeah, I saw him." Sarah stubbed her cigarette violently into the ashtray. "It's worse than ever."

Donna leaned forward. "Why didn't you tell me?"

"Oh, I don't know." Sarah said with contrived nonchalance. "I told Michael. I guess I forgot to tell you."

Donna's face darkened. She picked up her Zippo and snapped it open and shut.

Sarah felt a sudden twinge of remorse. She was being mean. It wasn't Donna's fault the ritual hadn't worked. She'd only been trying to help. She knew that Donna loved her. And she loved Donna, too. As for Peter, she had led him on that night because she was mad at Michael. Or confused. Yes, that's what she had been. *Confused.* She decided to lighten up, to stop being so serious and just resign herself to having a good time. She adopted a pleasant tone in her voice. "What were you trying to tell me earlier, before Peter showed up?"

Donna looked at her guardedly then visibly relaxed. "I'm getting a tattoo," she said.

"What and where?" Sarah asked, opening a new pack of cigarettes and offering the first to Donna.

Donna accepted the cigarette, lighting it with a quick snap of the Zippo. She blew smoke through pursed lips and raised her eyebrows the way she liked to do. She spoke in an Irish brogue. "Well . . . I thought of getting one of those little fighting leprechauns, you know, the ones with their fists in the air . . . for obvious reasons."

". . . because you wish you were Irish . . . and you like to fight . . ."

Donna pointed her cigarette at Sarah in validation. "Yeah. Then I thought about a shamrock."

"... for luck ..."

Donna pointed at her again.

"... and because you wish you were Irish ..."

"And then I thought about getting one of those ladies, you know, like Betty Boop or something, tattooed around my navel so I could make it dance and freak out little kids."

Sarah burst out laughing. She had forgotten that she had told Donna the story of her childhood "trauma" with the biker at the Gorge. Its high cliffs and trees were a perfect backdrop for pot smoking and lovemaking, the beach reserved for more open activities: children playing in ill-fitting bathing suits, parents reclining on elbows, squinting from sand-covered blankets; the mossy smell of water, damp towels, wet dogs. Mostly the bikers kept to them-selves, but sometimes, paths crossed, like at the concession stand. She had stood waiting for her order, balanced on one leg like a flamingo, rubbing the sandy sole of her foot up and down her shin. The coins were warm from the sun but cooler than her hand. There was the odour of oil and flour at the concession, the mingling sweet and acrid smell of ketchup and relish and vinegar. The light was glaring off the peeling white paint of the counter when the biker came, big, bearded, eclipsing the sun. She tried not to look at him, his belly bulging from a black leather vest, his arms decorated with a twisted rainbow of skulls and snakes and women's fiendish faces. But she couldn't look away as he turned to her, almost out of obligation it seemed, and began rolling his jiggling stomach in and out, like bread dough, the naked hula dancer at his navel shaking and rippling, ink breasts pointing up, then down, up, down. It made her feel so thin and hard and small ...

"As long as you don't get the Grim Reaper tattooed on your stomach and then run off and get pregnant," Sarah said.

"What are you talking about?"

"You know . . . that woman we met last year in the bar. The one with the weird tattoo on her stomach."

"Oh my God, right!" Donna guffawed. "She was all tough, getting inked with the Reaper, and then her stomach stretched all out of shape and she had to have it *transmogrified* into something."

"A dancing groundhog," Sarah said.

"No, it was a beaver."

"God, how macabre is that?" Sarah rolled the ashes from her cigarette, pushing them around the tray. "So what are you going to get?"

Donna took a long drag, speaking through the smoke in her affected brogue. "A beautiful little woodland sprite . . . on me ankle, don't you know."

Sarah nodded with approval. "I'm surprised. I would have thought a skull and crossbones. Doesn't the ankle hurt the most?"

"Yes, and I don't care. It's worth it." Donna eyed Sarah over the lip of her coffee cup. "Why don't you come with me?"

"No, I don't think so."

"Come on."

"I wouldn't know what to get."

"You don't have to know. You can decide when we get there. They have stacks of books to look through."

"It's expensive," Sarah said. "And isn't it supposed to be dangerous?"

"It's clean these days," Donna insisted. "They take precautions."

"Oh, well then," Sarah said. "As long as they take *precautions.*"

* * *

"It's an oak tree." Sarah winced as she peeled back a corner of the neat white bandage covering the tattoo on her hip.

Michael inspected the raw skin. "It looks more like the burning bush right now."

Sarah swatted at him, pressing the bandage back down. "You know what it's like. Your arm must have been a mess after your tattoo." She gave a little yelp of pain as she slipped her jeans back over her hips and zipped them up. She cinched her belt tight to hold her pants up, the tongue lolling out of the belt loop.

"The only thing I'm concerned about," Michael said, "is that I won't be able to manhandle you until your tattoo is healed."

"Guess not."

"I'm just going to have to resort to videos instead."

"Guess so."

"You don't even care."

"Guess not."

Michael lunged for her, stopping short as his hand gripped her wrist. He seemed shocked by the frailty of it, almost as if he was afraid he would snap it like a twig. He released her and ran his hand gently through her hair. "I can still kiss you, can't I? Or did that tattoo affect your lips as well?" He kissed her softly. "Why an oak tree?" he asked.

"I don't know," Sarah answered, her eyes becoming glazed and distant. "I've been dreaming about it lately . . . a tree just like it. The dream is always the same. I'm walking through the woods. It's dark. I can barely see my own hands in front of my face. But somehow, I know which way to go, like I've been there before, like it exists in my memory from child-hood or something. And then I see it—the oak tree. It stands out from the rest of the trees in the woods, like it's backlit, a bright light all around it. And it's as if I can feel it, like some-how I'm part of the tree. It wants me to come closer . . ." Her words trailed off.

"Hey," a voice said through the bedroom door. It was Michael's father. "How are you doing today?"

Michael turned back to the computer, silent. Sarah waved half-heartedly. "Hey," she said, clutching modestly at her shirt collar. She could feel his eyes examining her.

"You kids should get outside and get some fresh air. You're starting to look wan." He stood in the door for a moment longer, but thankfully disappeared.

Michael looked at Sarah. "So what happens?" he asked, as if his father had never been there.

Sarah sighed, pushing her hair behind her ears, her voice becoming flat and far away. "I don't know. Nothing, I guess. I just stand there and look at it. And then I wake up. It's the same every time."

He put his arms around her and kissed her face, brushing several loose strands of hair from her eyes. "I love your bangs."

"Why do you hate your mother?" she abruptly asked, pulling away from him.

127

Michael looked at her in momentary shock. "I don't hate her. I just don't respect her."

Sarah sighed. Wasn't that his way, to split hairs, to argue over the details? "Okay, why don't you respect her?"

"She was weak," he said, moving over to the computer and bringing John's file up. "She had no backbone. She couldn't stand up to the smallest challenge." He clicked the screen, made John's guitar shiver with motion. "Something happened between them at some point. I don't know what. But she wouldn't let him touch her any more—she couldn't stand the idea of his hands on her, hands that handled sickness and death. And then she left. He tried to kill himself," he confessed.

"Why?" Sarah gasped.

Michael shook his head. "I'm not sure. I think it was the weight of it, the burden of so much hopelessness. I think one of his patients had asked him for an assisted suicide and he couldn't do it. He couldn't face it. I don't know if he was thinking about killing himself, really, or just thinking about what it would be like to face death for real, the way his patients do every day."

"I'm sorry," Sarah said, ashamed that she had pushed the issue. "I guess we all have our skeletons in the closet."

"Some more than others."

She stared at him sympathetically, the question burning in her mouth. "How do you know he tried to kill himself?"

His hand stopped working the mouse as he sat back contemplatively in his chair. "I found him one night, sitting in his room. I surprised him. I wasn't supposed to be home but I skipped that day. He had the gun beside him, on the bed. I knew when I saw him what he was thinking before I even

THE BOOK OF LIVING and DYING

noticed the gun—just by the way he looked at me. I could
tell he'd crossed some line in his mind."

"God." It was all Sarah could think to say. Her family was
crazy, that was for sure, but no one had ever thought about
killing themselves—at least not to her knowledge, not
openly. Her mother's willing disappearance from society,
her spirit dissipating like rings of smoke in the air, that was a
suicide of sorts, she thought. But nothing like blowing your
brains out in your bedroom. That was so final, so desperate.
Her father . . . well, maybe he had thought about it some
night while driving alone in the middle of nowhere, along
some lonely ribbon of road, the dark pressing in on him.
Maybe. But he'd thrived on uncertainty, she knew that. As
long as he had a tank full of gas and a glass of scotch he could
be hopeful.

And then a memory of John imposed itself. Hadn't he
asked her to do it? Hadn't he asked her to find a way? Poison
would be his best friend in his hour of need, he'd said. It
would allow him to die with dignity. It would provide him
with choice. Promising to find a way, Sarah had begun
researching Hemlock societies and combing through ancient
herbal tomes for an appropriate agent. It was in a book
called *Gerard's Herbal* that she'd met belladonna, the plant
known as deadly nightshade, or *Atropa*. Called the enchan-
tress, the devil's herb, the most pernicious of the three fates,
her toxic berries were said to cause madness in small doses,
and in larger quantities "bring present death."

But John had abandoned the idea late in the game and
never mentioned it again. Sarah thought he'd gotten cold
feet, that he'd given up on the idea when the stark reality of
death became too certain to face directly. She'd been secretly

relieved by his silence over the issue. It let her off the hook; she wouldn't have to face the horror of it. And then she'd made it her reality, trying to understand what it would be like to be him. To know that death was just behind the door and that that door would inevitably open. Every motion, every gesture, tinged with the knowledge of death's approach. *I'm brushing my teeth; I'm dying. I'm tying my shoes; I'm dying. I'm combing my hair; I'm dying.* It wasn't until much later that she learned of how he had asked the doctor to do it, the doctor flatly refusing, saying it went against his Hippocratic Oath. *Maybe that's why he's haunting you,* she thought. Because he knew deep down that she didn't have the guts to end his pain—that she had gone through the motions but never really intended to help him at all . . .

Sarah yanked her mind back to Michael. It was much easier to think about someone else's problems. To be abandoned twice . . . what would that be like? First his real mother, then his adoptive mother. And then his father on the bed with a gun. It was so . . . screwed up. "I'm sorry," she said again. Then thought it was necessary to say more. "How did you handle that?"

"I didn't have to," Michael said, rather distantly. "He never mentioned it again so I left it alone. And that's where it stands. It wasn't his time, you know what I mean?"

What an awful thing to face, Sarah thought. What a terrible thing to carry in your heart. In a gesture of sympathy, she put her arms around him. She took his hands, guided him up and toward the bed. He hung back, dragging his feet, allowing her to coax him forward. She lay down on the bed and pulled him in beside her. One arm behind his neck, she cradled his head, sidling into him. She stroked his face, kissing him several times on the forehead. They lay together like that, until she thought that he was asleep, his breathing regular, light. Nuzzling her face against his, she let her fingers trail through his hair.

"I love you," he whispered.

A wave of gratitude washed over her. He loved her. *Her.* And she loved him, too. Desperately. All at once great joy and profound pain collided in her heart. How had they managed to find each other? How had their souls recognized their similarity, their common need? She traced the lines of his tattoo with her finger. He had given her so much. He knew things. Like the night he took her to the circle in the cedar forest and the stones that marked its place. Like a cemetery. Like the one in Terrace.

Where tombstones radiate outward, as the growth rings of a misshapen tree, so that the centre stones, being made of limestone, constitute the oldest, with rings of headstones expanding by years, the most recent located on the outermost ring, carved in granite. Pink and brown. Or black. The entire cemetery occupying ten acres, circumvallated by a stately wrought-iron fence possessing one main entryway by the groundskeeper's house, and two auxiliary gates on the north and south walls. Their plot was in the newest and final location, cremations only, past the Asians with their double-bed headstones, and to the right of the Jews. Some of the oldest trees in the state were located there, a climax forest of maple, beech and oak. It was a popular place for dog walkers and, oddly, lovers.

Because love conquers all, Sarah thought, kissing Michael's arm.

131

CHAPTER NINE

"Where are we going?" Sarah asked. She felt slightly nauseated and the sun hurt her eyes. She squinted out the passenger-side window of the Ford Escort, Donna's mother's car. It seemed incongruous, Donna in her combat boots and black rag-doll hair, nose ring glimmering, driving something as conservative as a Ford Escort.

"It's a secret," Donna said, shifting to a higher gear. Highway speed. "A Hallowe'en present. I've been meaning to take you here for a while." She fumbled with her cigarettes, pulled one out, tossed the pack on the dash and engaged the lighter. The car swerved slightly.

Sarah looked at her nervously. "Smoking is one of the major causes of automobile accidents."

Donna scoffed, popping the lighter out and holding it to the end of the cigarette, eyes lowered.

"Could you at least look at the road?" Sarah asked.

The car swerved again, tires crossing the white line. "Right," Donna said. She pushed the lighter back in its housing, took an affected pull on the cigarette.

"No, I'm serious."

"I'm watching the road, Wagner!"

"I mean about smoking causing accidents."

"Give me a statistic."

"I don't know."

"Come on." Donna snapped her fingers impatiently.

"It's high."

"How high?"

"I don't know, 50 percent, or something."

"What crap. It's that damn surgeon general. He's the bogeyman of the twenty-first century, disseminating false information to make people quit. Cancer, lung disease, death by second-hand smoke, asthma—car accidents, now."

Sarah frowned, taking a cigarette from Donna's pack. Pulling the car's lighter out, she looked at the grey metallic spiral of the element, then pushed it back into its housing. She waited for the pop, lit her cigarette and replaced the lighter. She exhaled, grateful for the distraction. "Well, if I'm going to die in a traffic fatality, I'd rather go down with my bloodstream full of nicotine."

"Amen." Donna made a motion with her hand toward Sarah, as though clinking a glass of beer in agreement.

The car rattled along the highway. They were well out of town now. The sun hung low in the sky. The trees along the highway stood like ranks of petrified soldiers, row on row, immobilized by some evil charm. They sped by in hypnotic rhythm as Donna chattered away about something, Sarah maintaining the conversation with low hums of agreement. She felt so tired. She rested her head against the cool glass of the window, the sun on her face. Just like that trip to Montreal. The last trip they ever went on as a family.

Her father boasting how he'd managed to get the best

room in the city, her mother's wooden figure in the passenger seat, noncommittal, terse. The first hotel was a total bust except that the kids had a room of their own. The stale smell of dirty laundry, the stiff sheets and flat pillows. She was thrilled when John—fourteen at the time—joined her in jumping on the bed, which they both did, wildly, until the plastic Shepherd casters supporting the frame snapped on one side, sending them careening and shrieking to their deaths on the orange molten lava carpet. Legs burned to charcoal twigs, eyes popping from their sockets. And then the horrifying discovery of the soiled diaper beneath the bed as her father kneeled down to inspect the casters. Her mother's disdain, her father's dark pride.

The next hotel vindicated him, with its picture window stretching across the room, high above the city, offering up the whole of Montreal for their pleasure. Wasn't it beautiful? Wasn't it just magnificent? Sharing the room, the four of them. And she, to her father's pleasure, begging to have the cot by the window so she could sleep like a sparrow, the city twinkling beneath her, until the fear of falling gripped her, more powerful than her father's unspoken disapproval as he dragged her cot to the middle of the room.

"We're almost there," Donna said.

They sailed past a road sign that announced the city of Salem, a silhouette of a witch flying on a broom as its logo. Beside the sign, on the gravel shoulder of the road, a faded plastic wreath perched on green wire legs. A crash site memento, Donna explained.

To the right of the road, the sun danced off the ocean, an endless silver expanse flashing in syncopated beats between buildings before the highway veered suddenly inland, carrying them to the centre of town.

Hallowe'en, and the place was a carnival. Tourists dressed as witches and vampires. Children in matching outfits. Even several dogs wearing black capes. Donna pulled the car into a parking spot on the street, cutting off a minivan that had obviously been waiting for the space to become available. The vampire driving the van cursed and sped off as Donna grinned and waved.

"They're so good-natured about the whole thing, aren't they?" she joked as they got out of the car. "Shall we do the tourist thing and grab a bowl of chowder at O'Neill's before our meeting?"

"Our meeting," Sarah numbly repeated. "I wish you'd tell me what this is all about."

"We'd better get off the street," Donna said. "We look like the weirdos dressed in our civvies."

O'Neill's was packed, the patrons costumed, animated. A group of vampires at a table near the window burst into raucous laughter.

"Looks like a scene from Hell," Sarah said as they stood in the entrance, hoping to catch a waiter's eye. Several bustled past, trays laden with frothy pints of beer and steaming bowls of chowder. They didn't even acknowledge Sarah and Donna.

"Hey," Donna shouted as a young waiter raced by, his cropped blond hair dyed pink, the sweat gleaming behind his ears. "Hey," she said again to no avail. "What do we look like? Chopped liver?"

Several witches glanced over with the smugness of patrons who are comfortably ensconced.

"Screw you," Donna sneered at them.

Sarah put her hand on Donna's arm. She didn't feel like a fight today. "It's okay. Let's go somewhere else."

Donna stood, glaring.

"We can go somewhere else," Sarah said again. "There are lots of places." She tugged on Donna's arm, pulling her from the bar into the street.

But it was the same deal in every other pub and restaurant in the city: harried wait-staff, fidgeting lineups, gleeful chatter from those who had managed to secure a table. So they wandered through the shops, also crowded. They sniffed essential oils and tried on hooded cloaks. They perused gemstones and crystals, bought saltwater taffy, had a boxing match with devil and nun puppets (Donna being the devil, of course), inspected rows of shot glasses and coffee mugs, all sporting the witch-on-a-broomstick logo.

"It's all just a pile of junk," Donna proclaimed. "They should burn this crap instead of witches. This is the real threat to America," she announced loudly, making a motion with her arm as if to clear the glass shelves of their merchandise. The shopkeeper eyed her warily. Donna gave her a satiric curtsy. "Let's pay our respects at the graveyard, shall we?"

The cemetery was crowded with "gawkers," as Donna called them. People with cameras and video recorders, little kids running around, playing tag among the tombstones, the limestone tablets leaning drunkenly. The gallows tree marked the centre of the small graveyard, its gnarled arms beseeching the sky. There was an unsettling energy, as if the ghosts of those convicted and tortured for witchcraft were reaching out, entreating the living to remember the hysteria that had led to the deaths of nearly two dozen people and the accusation and incarceration of hundreds more.

Donna clucked in feigned disapproval. "Best marketing gimmick ever. A few months of terror in 1692 translate into millions in tourist income. Not a bad trade-off."

Sarah shoved her hands in her pockets, kicking absently at one of the tombstones. She didn't want to think about the stupidity of the human race. People were awful at the best of times, she knew that.

"They're not all in here," Donna continued with a gleeful tone in her voice.

"What do you mean?"

"The bodies of the accused. They're not all in here." She bent down to read the inscription on a headstone. "The families weren't allowed to bury their dead. The bodies were just tossed in shallow graves and covered in dirt. And when it rained, you could see fingers and toes sticking out through the mud. So the families came at night, stole the bodies away and buried them in secret, in unmarked graves." She looked up at Sarah, smiling.

"You love that idea." Sarah shuddered, folding her arms across her chest. Thankfully John was cremated. Nothing but a pile of ash. Nothing to fight over. Nothing to push up through the mud. But it hadn't stopped his ghost from wandering around. And here she was on Hallowe'en, in the spookiest place in the world, at a time when spirits roam freely. Sarah watched as the children played among the tombstones, their hide-and-seek laughter filtering through the autumn air, her thoughts tumbling like a dropped penny. How different was she from Donna, really? Hadn't she stretched out in a pine coffin once on a school trip to Pioneer Village just to make her friends laugh? Eyes closed, hands folded neatly over her chest. She was suddenly irritated, suddenly impatient with the crowds, with herself, and most especially with Donna. "Why are we here?" she demanded.

But Donna ignored her. "We should go," she said.

"What's this stupid appointment for, anyway?" Sarah grumbled as they left the cemetery. Taking a shortcut through a side street, they walked past the shops on Essex to a narrow alleyway like a missing tooth in the row of red-brick buildings. The walls of the buildings were tall, threatening to pinch the space shut at any moment. Donna moved along the corridor, scanning the population of strange doors that lined the wall, some painted, some wooden, some with windows, some blind.

"It should be here somewhere . . ."

What kind of door? Sarah wondered, her mind latching on to a story by H. G. Wells, about a door in a wall. *"I am haunted. I am haunted by something—that rather takes the light out of things . . ."*

"This is dumb, Donna. Let's go."

"Here it is," Donna said, stopping in front of a weathered pine door. She checked the number: 17½. Testing the door handle, she wiggled it and pushed hard. A bell jingled flatly. The smell of incense and cigarettes hung in the air. A couple of dingy yellow upholstered chairs crouched in the dim light of the room, the dirty mustard walls decorated with faded moons and stars, the room truncated by a worn white curtain that hung from ceiling to floor at the back. Behind the curtain, a woman's voice could be heard, raspy, muffled. Donna slumped into one of the chairs. Sarah sat across from her, hands still shoved in her pockets.

"A fortune teller."

Donna nodded. "She's supposed to be good," she whispered.

When did Donna ever whisper? "Have you been here before?"

"She comes highly recommended," Donna said evasively.

She produced her cigarettes, reconsidered and slipped them back into her purse to fiddle with her Zippo instead.

Just then, the curtain was pulled back and a man appeared, looking embarrassed. He smiled nervously at Sarah, glanced at Donna and hurried out the door. A moment later a woman stood at the curtain. She looked at Sarah, her almond-shaped eyes black as coal. Like Michael's. She wore an old sweater and jeans. Her face was round and dispassionate, worn with abuse. Hardly the image of the all-seeing mystic, Sarah thought.

The woman motioned for her to come in and disappeared behind the curtain. Donna sat expectantly in her chair. What was that look she had on her face? Conniving? Delight? Sarah wasn't sure. She rose, hesitating at the sound of the woman's grating cough. Pulling the curtain back, she could hear Donna snapping her Zippo open and shut behind her. Open and shut.

The woman hunched at a tired orange melamine table, a deck of cards to one side, a cigarette burning in a nicotine-stained ashtray. A thin lamp leaned in one corner, the shade faded, ripped, strands of beads hanging from its craned neck. The smell of alcohol was overpowering. Gin? Rubbing alcohol? A metal chair with a wooden seat and back, the kind used in grade-school gynasiums, stood in front of the table. The woman motioned soundlessly to the chair. Sarah stepped into the room, letting the curtain fall closed. She could see the scuffmarks of a million encounters on the linoleum floor as she pulled the chair out and sat down.

The woman didn't speak. No small talk, no questions about why Sarah was there. Her wide, puffy hands were remarkably nimble as she began shuffling the cards. Tarot cards, Sarah could tell, now that she was closer. The woman began to cough again; the smell of alcohol and smoke made Sarah feel faint. There was barely enough room for the table and two chairs in the room, let alone the fumes radiating from the woman. Sarah covered her nose and mouth with one hand to keep the nausea down. The woman sucked her cough back with a long pull on her cigarette and continued to shuffle the cards, her face taking on a glazed, hypnotized appearance. Snapping cards on the table in the pattern of a cross, she studied them briefly. The name of each card was printed clearly across the bottom: ten of Swords, two of Cups, the Emperor, the Magician. She looked up at Sarah, looked through her, actually, her dark eyes focused on a spot far beyond the young girl in front of her. When she spoke, her speech was slow and thick with accent, her tongue clicking heavily in her mouth like a beetle.

"You are looking for the girl," she said.

Sarah shook her head, no.

"You are looking for the girl," the woman said again, then touched the card marked "The Emperor." "There is a man. He is of the world. He no longer serves you. You must leave him behind."

"Peter . . ." Sarah murmured.

The woman's eyes did not register acknowledgment. Her face remained vacant. "You are searching for an answer. A clue. The pieces are in front of you. They always have been." She held one hand lightly over the cards. "There is another man." She pressed a thick finger on "The Magician," the familiar lemniscate floating just above his head.

"Michael . . ."

"He has a message for you," the woman said, tapping repeatedly on the card. *"Je suis un mensonge qui dit toujours la vérité."*

140

Sarah waited for her to explain. "I'm sorry . . . I don't speak French."

The woman responded by flipping a card off the top of the deck and placing it into the middle of the cross: the Lovers. An edge of urgency tinged her voice. "Trust him," she said. She plucked another card off the deck, laid it across the Lovers: the Fool. It showed a man walking with a sack tied to a stick carried over one shoulder and a little dog running at his feet. He walked toward the edge of a cliff, his gaze turned heavenward, unaware of the danger before him. Raising her head slowly, the woman looked directly at Sarah, her eyes glittering in the dusky light of the lamp. Sarah stared back, unable to resist the impenetrable void in the woman's eyes as the final card was revealed: a black-armoured skeleton riding a white horse. Death. The woman leaned across the table, the smell of alcohol and cigarettes surrounding her like an aura. *"Bury your dead,"* she hissed.

The words scalded Sarah like steam from a burst pipe. In an instant, John was there, sitting across the table in the woman's place. Stomach lurching, Sarah hunched forward, the acid rushing into her throat. She covered her mouth with her hand as her head began to spin and she thought for sure she would be sick.

But when she looked up again, it was only the woman sitting across from her, gathering the cards and straightening the deck into a neat pile. Whatever spirit had possessed her was gone, her face dispassionate and empty once again. Sarah staggered back from the table, the legs of the chair scraping loudly against the floor. She stumbled, groping for the curtain, and was relieved to see Donna still waiting as she appeared from the back room, dazed.

Donna rose up and pressed something (a business card?)

into Sarah's hand before disappearing behind the curtain herself. Stuffing the card into her coat pocket, Sarah lunged for the door and pulled it open, the bell jangling as she stepped into the fresh air, the shadowed alley bright in comparison to the fortune teller's den. She breathed frantically in and out, felt the fumes of alcohol and smoke leaving her lungs, then heaved forward and retched, the vomit splashing loudly, astonishingly, against the bricks in the alley. Hands shaking, she searched her purse for a tissue and wiped her mouth, dropping the soiled tissue to the ground with disgust. She made her way down the alley, shivering uncontrollably. *Stupid old woman.* She exhaled forcibly, throwing her head back until she could see the robin's-egg-blue strip of sky. In a moment she heard the door close and Donna's footsteps tapping quickly behind her.

"Hey, wait up!"

Sarah walked faster.

"Hey," Donna said breathlessly. "What'd she say?"

"Did you pay her?" Sarah asked bitterly.

"Yeah, of course. What did she say?"

"I don't know."

"Come on, Sarah."

Sarah's voice rose with acrimony and confusion. "I mean it! I don't know. She didn't make any sense. She was speaking French, Donna." Sarah spat on the ground. "She's just a crazy old drunk. You wasted your money."

Donna nodded. "Yeah, well, it doesn't matter what she said."

"What?"

She lit a cigarette nonchalantly and offered one to Sarah.

Sarah turned away, running her hands over her face and through her hair. "Can we get out of here please?"

*   *   *

At least Donna knew enough to leave her alone on the trip home. Sarah pretended to sleep while Donna occupied her time fiddling with the radio, changing stations furiously whenever a song came on that she didn't like. From time to time, Sarah could feel her staring, desperate to talk but thankfully resisting the urge. She wanted to forget about the afternoon, the children in the graveyard, the smell of alcohol and cigarettes, the taste of vomit still lingering in her mouth, the woman's voice. Sarah tried to shut her mind to the words and the feeling of terror they sparked in her. But the woman's pronouncement hammered over and over in her head. *Bury your dead.* What had she meant by that? The look on her face, the conviction in her eyes. Those eyes. Sarah moaned lightly and swallowed. She squinched up her face, trying to block the images from playing out in her mind. But the dead weren't easily fooled, were they? Oh, no. The dead were tricky. Restless. First sign of rain and they were popping up like mushrooms, fingers and toes poking out of the mud like rotting carrots, desperate relatives sneaking around at night to cover them up again, hide the bodies, preserve the family name. And what was it that she had said in French? Something about a message?

Sarah started awake as the car rolled up to her house. She had managed to sleep after all. Donna was looking at her, her face half lit in the glow from the street lamp, the other half in shadow. Like Two-Face, Harvey Dent from *Batman*, Sarah thought. She laughed to herself. Michael had said that once about Donna.

"We can go somewhere for a drink," Donna offered. "If you don't want to go home right away."

"No, I'm so tired," Sarah said. She thought she saw something in Donna's face. An apology, maybe? Whatever it was, it was too late. She opened the door and stepped from the car.

Donna drove away as Sarah struggled with the key in the lock. The deadbolt resisted. The door wouldn't open. For one frantic moment she was convinced that it was John, holding the door handle from the other side. *"Don't freak yourself out,"* she told herself as she walked around to her bedroom window. Inching the frame up with her fingers, she squeezed her hands in the opening and pushed the window up. She tossed her bag onto the bed, stuck her head through for surveillance and crawled into her room. Once inside, she walked as bravely as she could to the bedroom door, opened it and looked out into the living room.

"Mom?"

The house was dark, except for the light from the street lamps casting ghostly trapezoids over the living-room floor. There was the familiar musty smell from the basement. It seemed stronger than usual. Sarah clicked on the light, banishing the trapezoids to the street. She sighed. The house was so small. Barely enough room for her and her mother, let alone any errant ghosts. Moving from the living room to the kitchen, she began turning lights on, calling out for her mother as she went. She even turned the light on in the bathroom.

A pile of dishes greeted her from the kitchen sink, a carafe of coffee cold on the element, the ashtrays—several of them—littered with cigarette butts. Sarah looked through the window in the kitchen door to the yard, expecting to see John staring back at her. But there was only the tangled silhouette of the locust tree near her side of the house. On the patio stones, an overturned lawn chair sprawled wantonly, several forgotten plastic tumblers littering the ground at its feet. Gathering her resolve, Sarah drew the curtain shut. She was spooked, that was for sure. She had even called out for her mother.

In the bathroom, she took the bottle of codeine and extracted two pills again, pushing the bottle to the back of the shelf afterwards. She held the tablets in her hand as she crouched in the kitchen, surveying the fridge. It stood under the counter, an old bar fridge her mother had scored at a second-hand store when their regular fridge went on the fritz. Sarah checked the contents. An open can of ginger ale, flat. Some margarine tubs containing mystery leftovers. Old celery wilting in the cracked plastic drawer of the vegetable crisper that magically turned everything to limp spaghetti. A few puckered tomatoes. It was worse than hospital food.

The lifeless vegetables, obviously frozen from a bag, the puréed mush in the morning posing as oatmeal, pale toast soggy with margarine. There were runs made to the deli and even McDonald's to compensate. It wasn't long, though, before food was no longer an option, the orderly stopping outside the door three times a day to check the charts at first, only to roll the food cart past the door and over to the next room. Within days the routine was established. There was to be no food of any kind delivered to 319. This was most difficult for the visitors, who had been used to arriving with cans of soda and bags of chips. It made the days seem even longer for everyone.

"Ugh," Sarah grunted, slamming the fridge door shut. The thought of food made her sick anyway. She took an etched whisky glass from the cupboard, the last vestige of her father, and turned the tap in the sink. After waiting several minutes for the water to run clear, she filled the glass. No ice. The bar fridge freezer didn't work. "Straight up," she said as she threw the codeine tablets back with a gulp of water. A wave of nausea swelled then receded. She refilled the glass and carried it to her room, the precise click of the door latch sharp against the quiet of the house.

Placing the glass on the milk crate, she lay down on the bed, listening. She was sure she could hear something. She strained her ears. It was the woman, crying faintly from somewhere in the house. Swinging her legs over the side of the bed, Sarah sat up and toed the corner of the rug that covered the trap door to the basement. She listened for a moment longer before getting up from the bed and inching the rug back slightly, then mustering her courage and throwing it to one side, exposing the plywood door.

The door was heavy. Her fingertips could barely pry it open and when they did, she could only lift it enough to stick her head into the dark hole. "Anybody down there?" The smell of damp and mould greeted her. With a whoosh of musty air, the door dropped back into its frame. Snapping the rug neatly like a bed sheet, Sarah replaced it over the plywood and lay back down on the bed. The picture of the skeleton on horseback glinted in her mind as she rubbed her forehead, praying for the codeine to kick in.

Outside, a low rumble rattled the window, followed by the erratic strobe of distant lightning. The tentative prelude of raindrops began, thrumming lightly against the glass, its ceaseless little hands searching endlessly. Fingers and toes sprouted spontaneously in Sarah's mind. She covered her eyes with the heels of her hands and held them there. Who can fathom the needs of the dead? The old woman's voice filtered through her thoughts. *You are searching for an answer. A clue. The pieces are in front of you. They always have been.* Sarah repeated the words, softly. She said them several times over, emphasizing a different word each time. What did it all mean?

The rain drummed harder, threatening to wash everything away. The way it had once at the hospital.

Pounding down with a force too great for the antiquated sewer system, causing the streets to flood. The bowels of the hospital eventually swelling with a brown soup, the rooms transformed, water cresting over gurneys and wheelchairs. Plastic bedpans floating with transparent snakes of medical tubing, boxes of wayward syringes bobbing along the surface like schools of skinny blue-nosed fish. An orderly, stripped down to his shorts, wading in to rescue a crate of bandages, despite the tears of one of the nurses who cried out in fear that he would be electrocuted. And the doctor, singing to all the patients about living in the belly of a whale.

Lightning lit up the room, thunder cracking menacingly on its heels. The lights in the house flickered. Sarah couldn't help thinking that it was John, trying to terrify her. If he was going to come, why didn't he just get it over with? She released the pressure on her eyes, dropping her hands with finality to her sides. Her fingers brushed against something in her jacket pocket. She felt around, pulled it out and held it up to her face. It was the card Donna had given her. Turning it over, she saw that it was a small photograph. A photograph of Michael and Donna. Together.

CHAPTER TEN

Sarah ran through the rain, the lightning hiccuping in fits through the sky, illuminating the trees in lurid flashes. Along the street, the houses hunched like sullen dogs in the downpour. She was soaked to the bone, freezing. Sneakers flopping, photo clenched in her hand, she splashed across the bridge to the park, the rain gushing in deep channels past her feet and swirling over the sewer grate on the other side. *"That witch!"* she spat through clenched teeth, thunder punctuating her words.

The park grinned wickedly in the storm, the lightning crackling along the hydro wires, snapping up the towers. The rain hammered down, icy fists hitting her skin. It pooled over the grass in electric puddles. Sarah ran toward the parking lot, sloshed over the slick pavement, skidded, swore when her knee hit one of the cedar posts that circled the lot like savage teeth, then continued to run. Slipping and sprawling along the jagged path, arms wheeling for balance, the muck running freely, splattering her legs and her face, she screamed before she even reached the top of the hill. "Michael!" She stepped on the rock beneath his window, sneakers squeaking as her ankle turned, sending her to the ground with a shout. She sobbed, the rain hitting her face, her chest heaving as she dragged herself up. Balancing on the rock again, she began smacking his bedroom window with her open hand. "Michael!"

When he did not appear the last of her reason was engulfed by incendiary notions of him with Donna, the two of them, together, plotting against her. She was searching for a rock to heave through the window when it clattered open.

"Sarah!"

She staggered back, reeling. "You liar!" she screamed.

His face disappeared from the window and in a moment he was running around the corner of the house, stopping short when he saw the look in her eyes.

"You liar," she sobbed, throwing the crumpled photo at him. It fell into the mud, the edges unfurling slowly like an odd flower.

Michael picked the photo up and looked at it, confused. He stepped toward her. "Please, Sarah, I never lied to you."

"Don't come near me," she warned, her eyes lit with rage.

"We never did anything," Michael insisted.

"I trusted you," Sarah wailed. She covered her face with her hands, the rain beating down on her, on both of them.

"Please, Sarah, it's a mistake . . ." He reached out to take her hand.

"Don't touch me," she cried. "Now I know why Donna hates you so much. She always said you were a creep. You must think I'm a complete idiot—a fool! Is anything you've told me true?"

"This doesn't mean anything, Sarah," he said, waving the photo in the air.

"It means something to me!" she yelled as she turned and plunged into the night.

She didn't stop running until she reached the bridge, her chest aching from the effort and the force of the rain. Heart jackrabbiting between hatred for Donna and contempt for Michael, she lifted her face to the sky, letting the rain pound her eyelids and lips. Now she understood the look on Donna's face in the car. She wanted Sarah to see what a conniving liar Michael really was. *Okay, you won,* she thought, her mind whirling with a mixture of torment and fury. *You won.*

And yet. And yet. Still the old woman's words would not leave her. *Trust him.* But who was the *him* that she spoke of? How could Sarah be sure? She felt so stupid, so ridiculously small. The Fool. Wasn't that one of the cards the old woman had set before her? Silly little fool. Pressing her fists into her temples, she let out a deep, frustrated yell, doubling over on the sidewalk, the rain gobbling up the sound. All she wanted was to be home, in her room, in her own bed. *But John could be waiting there.* The realization sent a shock wave of fear through her brain. "What do you want from me?" she howled. She crumpled onto the curb and stayed there until she was too cold and weary to care about ghosts, or broken promises, or anything else, and made her way home.

She noticed the wet footprints immediately, drying near the foot of her bed. His footprints. Grabbing a rag from under the kitchen sink, she furiously scrubbed the prints from the floor, her knees leaving their own wet marks, like dark sunbursts, where she had knelt. After, she slipped a roll of duct tape and a carving knife from the kitchen, taped her bedroom door closed, then waited, the knife blade glinting next to her in bed.

When she woke, to her horror, the tape was gone and so was the knife. Fighting back hysteria, she searched the room, beneath the bed, under the sheets. She even checked under the rug that covered the trap door. When she could not find the knife, she bolted into the kitchen, tearing open the drawers. The knife shone in the cutlery drawer, exactly as she had found it, the tape in its usual spot, one drawer down. Gaping in terrified disbelief, she convinced herself that it hadn't happened at all and kicked the drawers shut with her sock foot.

* * *

The sound of Mr. Kovski's voice was eroding her mind. It was almost as bad as the questions that dogged her waking hours and tracked her ceaselessly in sleep as well. How long had they known each other? Why hadn't Donna said something about Michael before? And what had made her decide to hate him? Sarah stared out the classroom window. She could feel Michael's eyes on her, the way they used to be before they had started seeing each other. Only now she wouldn't acknowledge him. She couldn't stand to see the pained look on his face, couldn't control the grenade blast in her skull whenever she thought of him with Donna. To stop the pain in her heart, she dug her fingernails into the palm of her hand. Would she ever learn the truth about the situation?

There had been a note slipped through the gills of her locker. She hadn't read it, hadn't even opened it in case she might be swayed to reconsider. In an act of bravado, she'd crumpled it, thrown it into the garbage as she'd walked to English class. Then thought about it all day. Thought about retrieving it and sneaking away to read it. It infuriated her that she cared. But she did. She couldn't deny it. Now she was sitting in calculus, waiting for the lesson to end.

It didn't surprise her to see Donna in class. Come to rubberneck the damage, no doubt. She wasn't striking her usual delinquent pose but was facing the front of the class, pretending to listen to the lecture. She hated that Donna had been right about everything. Hated the underhanded way she had used to expose Michael. She decided not to tell her about finding the photo. Let her sweat it out. The worst part was that Donna was being so nice, waiting at her locker, speaking in saccharine tones, tiptoeing around Sarah like she had just discovered that she was dying of some horrible disease. Wasn't that what happened with John? All at once, everyone treating him differently—his friends, her mother, the nurses and doctors—all speaking in falsetto, mincing around, as though he were a bomb about to explode.

Their expressions animated with feigned cheerfulness, quaking voices reaching for a higher timbre. Until eventually the strain wore the façade of levity away to reveal the true face of enduring grief.

Sarah thought of Michael, of everything that had happened between them: the video, the photo, his admission of love. Donna was jealous, she concluded. Wasn't that obvious? Still, there was the fly-buzz of doubt, the faint possibility that perhaps Donna knew something that she didn't, that she'd been acting the part of the good friend. Maybe Sarah had been wrong, dismissing Donna's concerns because she wanted to believe the best about Michael. It made her sick just thinking about it, the argument whirling around and around in her head until she thought she would scream. It would be easier to assume that Donna had acted out of jealousy. Michael couldn't possibly be interested in her, no matter what the photo implied. But he was a liar too, keeping such secrets from her. Maybe they were perfect for each other. This last conclusion nearly broke her.

She fingered her journal listlessly. She had tried to recall the old woman's words, writing down as much as she could remember. Recording the images as best she could. After class, she planned to do some research in the library to find the meanings of the cards. Looking down at her page, she saw that she had drawn dozens of spirals over the margins.

Mr. Kovski stopped to consider the brilliance of his last statement, then turned to the board to prove it in chalk dust. Sarah held her head in her hands. She was so tired. She could hardly keep her eyes open. If she could only put her head down, rest her face against the cool wood of her desk. She was thinking this when she became acutely aware that everyone was staring at her, including Mr. Kovski. He stood, chalk poised dramatically in the air.

"I'm sorry, what?" she asked.

"Are you feeling all right, Ms. Wagner?" he asked, icily. "You appear to be in some sort of distress."

The blush crept into her cheeks. "No, sir."

"No, you are not feeling all right?"

"No, I—I'm not in any distress."

"Good," he said. "I would hate to think that I was boring you."

She opened her mouth to speak but the bell trilled sharply.

"Stupid prick," Donna said as she stood over Sarah's desk crunching on an apple.

"Yeah," Sarah mumbled. She automatically glanced over at Michael, caught herself and turned her back to him. He would try to catch her at the door or at her locker. She would take evasive measures. She pushed her books into her knapsack, her journal slipping out and dropping with a low clunk to the floor. It flopped open, the pages fanning to her most recent entries.

"What's this?" Donna asked, retrieving the book from the floor.

"Nothing." Sarah grabbed for the book but it was too late. Donna was already studying her illustrations of the cards.

"'Ten of Swords,'" she read aloud. "Someone must have been pissed to stab this guy ten times in the back."

I know how he feels, Sarah thought grimly, reaching for the book again. Donna manoeuvred it just beyond her grasp. She bit the apple dramatically, chewing it loudly.

"The Magician. The Emperor. The Lovers. The Fool. *Death.*" She emphasized the last entry with a nod. "These drawings are pretty good."

"I'm glad you approve." Sarah snatched the book away and stuffed it into her bag.

Donna walked beside her, still eating the apple. Sarah noticed Michael standing at the end of the hall. Head lowered, she monitored the movement of her feet until she reached her locker. When she looked up again, he was gone. She felt the sharp pinch of disappointment but squelched it instantly with a slap of anger. That was the way to do it. That was how she would protect herself. Whenever she felt like forgiving him or seeing him again, she would kill those feelings with a carefully aimed shot of rage.

155

Donna crashed her locker open, throwing her books to the bottom. The half-eaten apple stuck in her mouth, she grabbed her coat and slammed her locker shut. She extracted the apple, wiping her mouth with the back of her hand. "Cup of j at Her Majesty's palace?"

Sarah regarded her coolly. "No, I don't think so. I've got work to do."

"More cards to draw?"

"Maybe."

"Come on. I'll buy."

"No, thanks, Donna."

"Maybe later? After you've finished . . . *your work*?"

Sarah detected a hint of sarcasm in her voice and made a mental note of it. A scorpion can't hide its true nature. "Sure, maybe later," she agreed, putting on her coat. "But don't wait for me," she added, slinging her knapsack over her shoulder and securing her locker.

✳   ✳   ✳

"I'm looking for books on tarot cards," Sarah said in a low voice.

The librarian sat primly behind her desk. She didn't look up but continued to type on her computer, her mahogany hair scraped back in an orderly bun, like a nurse, her tortoiseshell glasses reined with a burnished silver chain and balanced fastidiously at the end of her nose. "Occult section, second floor," she answered, rather loudly.

Sarah winced, pushed away from the desk and moved through the congregation of books toward the stairwell, past the liquid eyes of old men reading newspapers draped like medieval tapestries on polished oak rods, through the quiet hum of information, the hush of people thinking, of order and antiquity, the scratching of pens on paper—the unacknowledged sounds of everyday things.

The efficient tapping of shoes down polished halls, the bell from the nurses' station, the clatter of laundry carts. The intermittent ding *of the elevator, its doors opening with a low* whoosh. *The voice of a patient crying out. An audible sigh. The resonance of dreams relinquished and forsaken.*

Sarah preferred the public library to the one at school. It was bigger, older. Steeped in history. It even had a ghost of its own. Some jilted lover hanged from one of the beams in the widow's walk, the stairwell to the walk boarded over for decades since. At least, that was the story all the students told. Even with the ghost it afforded more privacy than the library at school with its prying teachers and nosy students. There was no Internet access at either library, though. She could have surfed the Net at Michael's if she hadn't been on the outs with him. She felt the knife jab in her heart. No. Books would have to do.

Climbing the stairs, she had to stop several times on the way up to catch her breath. The oak door greeted her at the top, offering a bevelled fly's-eye view of the floor. The brass handle was cool to the touch. She eased the door open, using her shoulder to brace it so she could slip through. The door closed heavily behind her, the vacuum lifting several papers from a desk against the wall with its breath. A girl from Sarah's media arts class sat perched on a wooden chair to the immediate left, whizzing through microfilm.

Slipping noiselessly into one of the aisles, Sarah hid behind the books and spied as the girl cranked the black plastic reel on the projector, the history of Terrace playing out in old newspaper images flashing dizzyingly across the screen. The idea of spying on her fellow student caused her to giggle uncontrollably. Michael would find it funny, she thought, and was at once overcome with grief. How could he have betrayed her?

She let out a small moan, ducking guiltily behind a stack of books when the girl looked over. Sarah crept low between the shelves for several rows before standing upright and walking, one finger cruising gently over the spines, stopping for a moment to withdraw and inspect a book on trees, then replacing it. She continued until she reached the section marked "Occult." Most of the books were well worn, the spines wrinkled with use. A hardcover entitled *Sabbats* caught her eye. She cracked it open. There were pages missing, the photos and important bits removed with a razor blade. "Nice," Sarah said, returning the book to the shelf and pulling out another. Again, pages carefully removed. "Haven't you heard of a photocopier, you jerk?" As she said this, she noticed a familiar title leaning to one side at the end of the shelf. It was *The Book of Living and Dying*, with its worn black cover and white bone lettering. Sarah gaped in disbelief, as though she had just witnessed an impossible sleight of hand. *How could this be?* She quickly chose two others and, holding them furtively against her chest, searched for a study carrel.

All the desks along the window were full, the students bent in intellectual labour. Past the window seats in the corner by the bathroom there was an empty carrel. Not her favourite place, but it would do. Placing the books on top of the desk, she pushed her knapsack underneath at her feet. On an impulse she pulled her chair off to one side so that her back was facing the aisle, concealing the tarot books, then instantly changed her mind. Why should she care if anyone knew she was reading books on tarot? There were lots of girls her age who were into the craft, into the metaphysical.

A deck of tarot cards fanned across the cover of the first book. Sarah flipped impatiently through the pages. It was some type of history of the cards, with very little written on their intended meanings. She shut the book and pushed it to one corner of the desk. She opened the next. *The Tarot Deck.* Each page showed an illustration of the cards with a written description underneath. Sarah flipped to the front, started to skim through the tiny print and immediately experienced the downward slide of defeat. It seemed that tarot readings were more complicated than she'd imagined. It wasn't just the meanings of the individual cards that mattered; a proper reading took into account the influence of the cards on each other. To make the situation worse, the order of the cards had to be considered as well as their orientation, either right-side up or upside down.

Sarah threw the book down in disgust. She couldn't remember in what order the cards had fallen, whether they were upside down or not. Now she would never know their true meanings, no matter how much she read. She tapped her pen against her journal, tossed it down and thrummed her fingers on the paper. Opening the book again, she turned angrily through the pages, stopping at the Magician. The illustration showed a young man in a robe, infinity symbol hovering above his head, one hand outstretched and lowered, pointing, the other raised, clasped around some two-ended object like a short staff. There was a chalice on a table in front of him, a sword, a stick of sorts and a circle with a pentacle. A tangle of flowers grew in the foreground: lilies, roses, some kind of vine. Sarah compared the illustration to the one in her journal, adding in the details she had overlooked or missed. When she was finished drawing, she read the description.

"Skill, diplomacy, self-confidence, will. Reversed: mental disease, disgrace, disquiet."

Mental disease. A spectre rose to the surface of her imagination and rolled languidly over. Michael's father on the edge of the bed, gun gleaming, its dire promise proffered in metal. The twitch of a finger, a single sharp syllable between here and the hereafter. She thought about John and his request.

The doctor standing nervously at the side of the bed, eyes averted. Hands stuffed in pockets. The body language of disapproval and refusal.

Something similar had pushed Michael's father over the brink, sent him crawling toward the redemption of a bullet. She decided that she would never tell Michael the terrible thing that John had asked. She didn't want to connect herself to him in that way, didn't want the weight of John's illness associated with his father's spiritual dilemma. Besides, she thought, justifying her feelings, how could she be sure the story about the gun was even true? A picture of Michael and Donna asserted itself in her mind. Of him kissing Donna, the way he had kissed her. Sharing laughter. The intimacy of discovered commonality. Had he made a video of her, too? Laughing bitterly, she whipped through the pages of the tarot book, stopping only when she reached the Fool, because she was sure that card had somehow represented her, and because she couldn't bring herself to explore the meaning of the black-armoured skeleton on horseback—yet. She read the description, her eyes resting on the final word: *nullity*. Something null, ineffective, characterless. What did any of it have to do with her?

Jumping up from the desk, Sarah shoved her journal into her knapsack. There would be no more reading about tarot today. There would be no more reading about it ever. It was all so pointless. The spark of anger flashed in her heart again at Donna, for what she had done. Putting ideas in her head, forcing her to examine things. All because she wanted to expose Michael for the fraud that he was. Sarah knew that she should be angry with him, too, knew that it was he she should be hating. But she didn't feel that way. The truth was, she missed him, terribly. It was Donna that she wanted to hate. *Shoot the messenger.* Wasn't that the way it worked?

A low, animal groan worked its way from her throat. The whole situation was so awful. But standing there, next to the study carrel, she vowed not to succumb to feelings of loneliness, no matter how much she longed to be with Michael. "I won't see him. I hate him," she said aloud. Several students turned to look at her. At once she was aware of her surroundings, aware that she was not alone. Trotting between bookshelves, Sarah wove her way back to the "Occult" section. The book was still there, and it seemed now that it was somehow mocking her. Snatching it up, she stuffed it behind the other books on the shelf, then ran to the stairs and padded down the worn marble steps, the soft *shush shush* of her sneakers punctuating the solemn hush even as she stepped into the frosty night.

*   *   *

Every bulb in the house was burning. Sarah lay in bed. No knives or tape this time. But it was lights on from now on. She was in control of the situation. Sheer will would overcome her fear. But what of her thoughts of Donna and Michael? They needed to be controlled as well. They were devious, sprouting full blown from the fertile soil of her mind. Time to weed that garden. Pull those nasty thoughts out by the roots. She took several codeine tablets, washing them back with the glass of water she now kept by the bed at all times. She knew she would have to take more soon to make it through the night; her tolerance to the medicine was growing. That was the way it worked.

The nurses slowly increased the dosage of morphine to keep step with the advancing pain. They made careful calculations. The blue cap popping neatly from the needle, its silver tip puncturing the intravenous tube to administer its reward. The needles were eventually abandoned altogether for the efficiency of a pump when the dosages got too high, the smooth plastic button resting just beneath the thumb for ease and unlimited access. Concern over addiction and self-control was no longer an issue once death became a certainty, the nurses depressing the pump on schedule when fatigue and fantasy led to forgetfulness.

❊   ❊   ❊

Sarah woke to find John hovering in the doorway again. Trying to quell her pounding heart, she closed her eyes lightly so that she could watch him undetected. He took a couple of halting steps toward the bed and reached for her, then brought his hand to his face in a posture of misery. Sarah scrunched her eyes shut, said a desperate prayer in her head. *Make him go away.*

* * *

There was another note in her locker: *"Please let me explain."* And then another. *"It meant nothing."* Sarah crumpled the notes unceremoniously, and discarded them. She took pains to avoid Michael, changing seats in class so that she wouldn't have to look at him, wouldn't be tempted to so much as glance in his direction. Once, while rushing out of school, she bumped into Peter. She smiled before she remembered to frown and was disappointed with herself for slipping up. His face was hard and unyielding, giving her nothing. She started avoiding Donna, too, preferring to read at the library (she didn't divulge this information) or to go home and lie in bed, her thoughts slipping through the weave of her blanket, in and out, rising and falling with the pattern, the hundreds of little loops and holes of the cotton thread occupying her endlessly.

The great expanses of time where no one arrived, elastic lengths of time that seemed to stretch on and on for days, when, in fact, it had only been hours in between visits. Lying on the bed, TV blinking, knees up, knees down, curled to one side, pillow squashed between bony thighs. The patient drip of intravenous measuring the moments like water on stone. The disease, equally ceaseless, working its way by undetected

*increments, moving silently among the blood cells bumping
like small cars through the veins, filtering deeper.*

Sometimes Sarah would raise her knees, forcing moun-
tains into her blanket landscape just to see how the shadows
would change things. At night she kept vigil, senses honed
to the slightest variance in sound. When she did manage to
sleep, her dreams were occupied by the girl and the oak tree,
or confused by the sound of the woman crying. She thought
she saw John, too, in fleeting glimpses, outside the room,
beside the bed, in shadows, breaking the light that glowed at
the base of the door. In a codeine-driven state she even
dared him to appear, but a gold-and-green beetle arrived
instead, made its way painstakingly across the floor to disappear mysteriously behind her slipper.

And still the notes persisted.

*"I'm working on a secret project. Don't you want to know
what it is?"*

"I love you."

And finally,

"It is finished."

Sarah mulled this one over. She didn't crumple it, but
slipped it into the side pocket of her knapsack. She knew
what it meant. She was weakening, she knew that too, her
rage diminishing like the sound of the chords she used to
strum on John's guitar, just the suggestion of it now, the
vibrations resonating in the air around her. Besides, anger
was exhausting. It took too much energy—something she
seemed to have very little of.

✳   ✳   ✳

Sarah stood on the street across from the library. She was too tired and restless for books so she turned back toward town instead. She would walk past the Queen's, just to look in. After cutting through the parking lot of the school, she came around the corner of the building and saw a group of men standing at the far end of the alley. Hesitating, she wondered if she should go around before realizing it was Michael in some kind of altercation with Peter and his friends.

She heard Peter say, "What are you going to do now?" then saw him shove Michael backward, sending him stumbling over his knapsack.

"Hey!" Sarah shouted. Peter glanced at her, then shoved Michael again. "Hey!" she yelled louder. She dug in her purse for her cellphone and held it in the air. "I called the cops, Peter!"

Peter lit out with his friends, but not before kicking Michael's knapsack across the alley. "Next time it will take more than your girlfriend to save you," he warned.

Sarah ran over to where Michael was standing, brushing himself off. She picked up his bag, wiped the dirt off and handed it to him. "Are you okay?" she asked.

He didn't look at her but took his knapsack, slung it over his shoulder and spat on the ground. Pulling a squashed pack of Marlboros from his bag, he inspected it ruefully, then pulled a cigarette out and lit it with a small green disposable lighter he produced from his pants pocket. He offered the pack to Sarah, who eyed it suspiciously. "It's okay," he said, acidly, "they won't explode."

"Since when do you smoke?" she asked, taking a rumpled cigarette and trying to straighten it before putting it to her lips. "And since when do you smoke Marlboros? That's my brand."

Michael shrugged and engaged the lighter, holding the flame up to Sarah's cigarette. "Did you really call the cops?"

Sarah tossed him the phone. He looked at it, pressed a few buttons.

"It's broken," she said. "It hasn't worked for a while. I just keep it for old times' sake."

He tossed it back to her. "Well, I, for one, am glad you had it. But if that little prick had the balls to fight without his army of mutants, I wouldn't need you to come to my rescue." His voice softened. "Let me buy you a coffee." He looked at her hopefully, saw that she was going to decline. "Or how about a drink, or a sub, or something . . . I know, a new cellphone . . ."

Sarah forced herself not to smile. "I'm still mad at you, you know."

He nodded. "I know. But I always make an effort to buy off the people who save my life . . . At least let me show you John's video. It's done and I think it's good—if I do say so myself."

"Can't you just bring it to school for me?" Sarah asked, trying to puff nonchalantly on her cigarette.

"Come on, Sarah." He stood in front of her. "I promise to tell the truth, the whole truth and nothing but the truth."

"So help you God?"

He raised his hand in burlesqued oath. "So help me God. But we should go—in case Peter and his merry men figure out the cops aren't coming."

He turned toward the street but Sarah stopped him with a hand on his arm. "Let's take the back way," she said. She didn't want to risk Donna seeing them together. She felt guilty. Guilty for allowing her resolve to be so easily eroded. Guilty for being afraid to be alone. But she couldn't help herself. She didn't want to end up like them.

The forgotten chronic care patients, dispossessed and doomed to measure out their final dreary days in prescribed doses. Few visitors called on the residents in the rooms of the west wing's third floor. Except for Room 319. There was almost always someone there, playing cards, chatting, sitting quietly and reading, working crosswords or word finders. But it soon became evident that visiting a resident in chronic care was not an exclusive experience, with patients looking eagerly on from wheelchairs, or propped up in beds by hallway windows, or even standing in the doorways of their rooms. More than once she had stopped to help a patient in distress, cover an exposed torso with pants that had slipped open and rumpled impudently to the ground, adjust a blanket that had lodged itself in the spokes of a wheelchair or just say hello to those in desperate need of company—in particular, Mr. Ellis next door in 317. She had started making rounds, like the doctors, to try to quash some of the loneliness. She wished Mr. Ellis wouldn't moan the way he did, his haunting voice high and detached, floating through the halls, calling for absent relatives too weary or uncaring to shoulder the burden of his illness, a ghostly hand shadowed against the white curtain, clawing to pull the fabric back. "I'm pining. I'm pining away in here. Tommy, Tabitha, will nobody come and talk to me?" Then calling out the lyrics of an old love song, his spiritless voice unbroken by cadence. Until she would appear and pull back the curtain so that he could see the world around him, his voice vanishing mysteriously in the air.

CHAPTER ELEVEN

"We met at a party," Michael said. He took a sip of his drink, stared at the ice.

Sarah clung to the edge of the bed, the codeine-and-alcohol cocktail washing over her. "What party? When?"

"Some out-of-town thing a while ago—a hemlock party. I got roped into going."

She shot him a look of disgust. "A hemlock party? That's not even funny, Michael. What was Donna doing there?"

He swirled the ice in his glass, took another sip. "I don't want to sound like a jerk or anything, Sarah, but she was all over me, you know? I wasn't really attracted to her."

"Why wouldn't Donna tell me about this?" Sarah said, more to herself than to him. The whole thing just didn't make sense. If only she could stop the room from spinning she might be able to figure it out.

"Maybe she was embarrassed about it once she sobered up," Michael said.

Sobered up? Sarah fixed him with a clinical gaze. "Did you make out?"

"Come on, Sarah."

"Did you make out?"

"I don't know!" He threw his drink back, unscrewed the lid on the brandy and filled his glass again.

"So, you're telling me you don't remember."

"No, I don't. I don't remember anything from that night."

"Don't remember anything . . . ? I find that hard to believe."

"I swear to you, Sarah. It's one big blur. I didn't even know she had that photograph. It's pretty weird, don't you think, someone carrying a piece of you around like that."

Sarah brought her glass unsteadily to her lips. "Kind of like finding a pirate video of yourself doing something you never did?"

"Yes—no—come on, Sarah, what can I say? There's nothing between us. The whole thing is just a coincidence. How can I make you believe that?"

"I'd just like to know why Donna thinks you're such a creep."

Michael contemplated his drink as though he expected to find an answer there. "At the risk of sounding egotistical," he finally said, "she wouldn't be the first girl to get pissed off for being ignored."

"What do you mean?"

"I mean, women have a tendency to get vindictive when they don't get what they want."

"And men," Sarah added softly, thinking of Peter. The brandy burned on the way down as she took another gulp from her glass. Michael's face moved in and out of focus. Yet even as she struggled to keep his features in place, she had to admit that she felt better just being with him, despite everything. She raised her glass in a sardonic toast, slurring the words. "To life—whatever it may be."

Tapping her glass lightly with his, Michael leaned forward

and spoke in a voice like Humphrey Bogart's. "Life ain't fair, sweetheart. That's all there is to it. So we drink our sorrows away and kick the guy next to us because it makes us feel better to know that someone hurts more than we do." He drained his glass, poured another.

"That's why there's the Island of Misfit Toys," Sarah said, placing her hand on his arm, ". . . so the misfits can stick together when the world rains down on their heads."

They roared with drunken laughter until Sarah sloshed her drink down onto the desk and gripped her head in her hands. "God, I feel so sick." She teetered on the edge of the bed, peering up at him through one eye. "What kind of a name is Mort?"

"It's pronounced *More*," he said, correcting her. "It's French. It was my mother's maiden name. I assumed it to honour my heritage."

Sarah furrowed her brow as if pondering an impossible question. "I thought your mom was native."

"She was. A lot of natives mingled with the French, if you know what I mean."

"So what's your 'father' called?" She mimed quotation marks with her fingers.

"Field."

"Field . . . Field . . ." Sarah rolled the name over her tongue. *Dr. Field*. The meaning of it kicked her square in the teeth. He was one of John's attending physicians. The patient who asked for an assisted suicide; the doctor who refused. So she and Michael were inextricably linked through a question and the answer of a gun. It was too remarkable a connection for mere coincidence and yet she couldn't bring herself to tell him. It was just too tragic, too sad for words. Sarah reached into her knapsack and tugged her journal out. "I want you to look at something." Leafing to the tarot entries, she handed the journal to Michael, pointing emphatically at the drawings of the cards. "What does it mean?"

Michael took the book, glanced at the illustrations. "These are good."

"Read that line," Sarah said, stabbing at the page. "Something in French. I have no idea what it means."

Michael handed the journal back to her. "The cards are just symbols, Sarah. They aren't meant to be taken literally. They're tools . . . to help people access the subconscious."

"She spoke French to me," Sarah persisted, pushing the book back at him. "Something about a message."

Michael took the journal and stared at the page. "It's not about a message . . . it's something else." He stood up, staggered across the room and pulled a thick paperback from the bookshelf—*Harrap's French/English Dictionary*—then sat down heavily on the bed, searching through the book. "'*Mensonge,*'" he said. "Is that the word she used?

"Yeah, that's it!"

"It means 'lie,'" Michael explained. "She must have been quoting Jean Cocteau. He was a French poet—and a notorious opium addict I might add. '*Je suis un mensonge qui dit toujours la vérité.*' I am a lie that always speaks the truth."

"A lie that always speaks the truth . . ." Sarah whispered the words. It was Michael the old woman was referring to. It had to be. *Trust him.* "She told me I was looking for the girl. Why would she say that?"

Michael tossed the journal onto the bed. "Why do you think she would say that?"

Sarah's mind drew a blank. "Maybe she meant the girl from the photos . . . I don't know."

Michael massaged his eyes with one hand, saying nothing.

Sarah felt suddenly embarrassed. She had let herself get carried away. She had made too much of it. *He'll think I'm crazy,* she thought, the codeine and alcohol opening the door to self-doubt. "I thought you were going to show me the video," she said, in an attempt to right the situation.

Michael sat down in his chair. Taking a small stool from the side of the desk, he motioned for Sarah to sit beside him. "You're going to like this. But first, I want to do something." Holding the offending snapshot between two fingers, he lit it with the disposable lighter, turning it so the flames swallowed the photo completely, before dropping it into the ashtray next to his bed. The edges curled and crinkled in on themselves, the flames flaring up in a prism of chemical colour, then vanishing. He turned to her, and in a show of fidelity, kissed her tenderly.

"Now," he said, clicking the mouse and opening a window so that John appeared on the screen, "Utopian Planet" grinding out over the speakers. His image flickered, moving around the imaginary landscape, sometimes wearing sunglasses, sometimes not. Birds flew from the guitar, grass and trees sprang up, flowers bloomed, the sky swirled with brightly coloured clouds, gathering, contracting.

"It's beautiful . . ." Sarah said, her lips still tingling from his kiss. "Is this the secret project you were working on?"

He shook his head. "No. I'm not finished with that yet. But soon."

She knew better than to press him. He wouldn't reveal his secret until he was ready. But watching John on the screen, she was immediately overcome by how much she loved him. Reaching for her glass, she promised herself that she would hold on to that feeling, that he would always be her brother, no matter what. Ghosts and all.

*   *   *

She couldn't find her house keys. Searching frantically, she found the keys eventually in the jumble of junk at the bottom of her purse. But the lock refused to cooperate. "Open!" she growled, rattling the key until the mechanism finally gave way and the door swung wide. Stepping quickly inside, Sarah raised her eyes just in time to see John float into her bedroom. She dashed back out, pulling the door shut behind her. Gasping outside the house, one hand still on the door handle, she thought to run back to Michael's, to sneak through his bedroom window and hide out there for the night. But then indignation reared up, and instead of running away, she barged into the house with a shout, only to find her mother waiting on the other side.

"What do you think you're doing?" her mother demanded.

Sarah ignored her blistering stare, busying herself with her shoelaces, putting her slippers carefully on her feet, adjusting her coat on the hook—anything to avoid acknowledging her mother. When her mother left her alone at last, Sarah crept up to her own bedroom and peeked in. It was empty. At least, from where she was standing it looked empty. She made her way into the kitchen, filled a tumbler with water from the tap and brought it into her room, dipping her fingers into the water and flicking them in mock exorcism. "Stay out," she commanded. After, she hunted around for a magazine because she knew that fear would prevent sleep from coming—even with the lights on.

*   *   *

The fist of nausea gripped her stomach. Sarah staggered out of bed and ran to the bathroom. Her body heaved repeatedly as the waves rode one on top of the other, her hands clenching the sides of the cold porcelain bowl. Outside the bathroom, her mother shambled haltingly through the kitchen, pausing to listen at the door. Sarah tried to retch quietly so that her mother wouldn't pry and jump to some stupid conclusion, like that she was pregnant. Ever since Sarah's first period her mother had worried endlessly that she would get in trouble. Sarah simply refused to entertain the notion, even though she knew it was a distinct possibility. She was weeks late. She wouldn't think about it, though. She just wanted to be sick in peace. But even as she hung her head over the bowl, hands trembling, dry heaves wrenching her body, she knew that illness of any kind was not a private affair. Illness was a spectator sport, it seemed.

It made it difficult to maintain even the smallest degree of modesty. Closed doors were strictly forbidden to allow free access for hospital personnel, who would burst in a thousand times a day asking about this and that, taking blood pressure, taking blood. And there was no such thing as a good night's rest, either, not with the living dead wandering the halls at all hours, or nurses crashing in to perform their rounds. Not a night went by that someone didn't have a major malfunction, like trying to climb into bed with one of the other patients or screaming at the top of their lungs because they believed that someone had taken up residence in their room, when they weren't in their own room in the first place. But the worst nights were the ones when death arrived, the dull bell sounding at the nurses' station, the quick squeak of white sneakers on the green linoleum floor.

The sudden appearance of relatives, clamouring down the hall, their cries of horror and grief. And then the stretcher, rolling soberly past the open doors of the other residents, sheet draped carefully over the dearly departed.

When the worst of it was over, Sarah wiped the saliva from her mouth with a damp facecloth. Taking several codeine pills from the bottle, she didn't worry any more that her mother would discover them missing. As she closed the medicine cabinet, though, her heart gave a momentary skip of fear at the thought of John's face reflected there. She surveyed her own face in the mirror: a weary, wooden mask. Her lips were chapped and cracked, like an old woman's. *It's his fault,* she thought as she picked up the hairbrush and began slowly brushing her hair. It came out in small clumps that dropped from her fingers into the wastebasket like little birds' nests, empty and forgotten. She continued to brush, until the pills started to take effect, anaesthetizing her brain and easing the fluid back into her joints. She would go to the cemetery, she casually decided. She would bring flowers.

✲   ✲   ✲

The cemetery was deserted. Sarah drifted along the path, a bright bouquet of orange chrysanthemums clenched in her hand. They were such happy flowers. At the hospital she had kept some by the bed always. She hunched her shoulders against the cold, dried leaves the colour of tobacco rolling like small tumbleweeds past her feet. The sky hung grey and heavy in the frosty air, the promise of snow lining the clouds gathering on the horizon. Along the path, trees leaned over, fingers woven in a tangled canopy above her head. The wind gusted in quick bursts. Sarah turned the collar up on her coat, fastening the button. She yanked a blue wool scarf from her pocket and shook it out, wrapping it around her neck and up over her chin, tucking the ends in at the throat.

The path twisted and turned through the graveyard. From time to time Sarah would stop to read an inscription. "One under heaven." She liked that one especially. She would insist on having that on her own headstone some day. With that thought, she wished that Michael were with her, sharing the tranquility of the cemetery. Standing among the tombstones, she felt the urge to kiss him, because he would understand her desire to be there and because she loved him. It amazed her how strong this feeling was and that it miraculously extended to the rest of the world as well—including her mother. This fascinated her, given the fact that she hadn't felt anything short of disdain for the woman for so long. All at once Sarah realized that she could never survive without Michael, that her life and his life were now forever entwined. The thought of him with another girl, she couldn't bear it—especially if that girl was Donna. She wondered again about his videos. She'd never considered checking to see if Donna was in any of them. The next chance she got, she would do that, though the idea filled her with humiliation. Her insecurity. Her lack of faith. But she couldn't be rational when it came to him. She'd lost too much already. There was no way around it. She would have to know for sure.

As Sarah turned back to the path, she was taken by the figure of an old man sitting on a bench in the distance. He sat staring straight ahead, a fedora over his silver hair so that he looked—profiled sharply against the grey sky—like a Victorian paper silhouette. Curiosity got the better of her and she stopped to watch him, the chrysanthemums held in front of her like a nosegay, when all at once the old man turned and looked at her. Sarah cried out, hiding quickly behind a large tree at the side of the path. The man was the spitting image of Mr. Ellis, the old man from Room 317. But it couldn't be him, she told herself. Mr. Ellis was dead. She'd seen it with her own eyes. Her breathing shallow and erratic, she covered her mouth with her hand. It couldn't be Mr. Ellis, she told herself again. It was just an old man enjoying the solitudè of the cemetery, perhaps musing on his life or the life of his loved ones buried there. But this tenuous rationale was quickly unmoored by the tide of delirium rising inside her, until she finally burst out from behind the tree, the chrysanthemums tumbling in an orange riot to the ground and trampled beneath her feet as she ran toward the street. She didn't dare look back to see if the man was still on the bench. It must have been the light, she convinced herself as she hurried along the sidewalk. The light, playing tricks with her eyes. She pulled the scarf tighter around her neck and quickened her pace toward home.

✻   ✻   ✻

"The *Collins English Dictionary* is the only dictionary I reference," Donna stated primly. She held the book up, running her hand seductively along the spine like a game show hostess. She read the copy off the jacket in a light, officious voice. "It's the most comprehensive single-volume dictionary on the market, with 170,000 references, 1,800 pages and 15,000 encyclopedic entries. The thumb index makes it especially easy to use, and it contains all my favourite lexico-graphical obscenities. Take this, for instance." She thumped the book open on the table, made a dramatic show of using the thumb index, then licked her finger and leafed to the page she was seeking. "'Fuck about,'" she said with school-marm prudishness. "'Offensive taboo slang. 1. to act in a stupid or aimless manner. 2. to treat someone in an incon-siderate or selfish way.'"

"Interesting," Sarah said. She threw a card on top of the pile. "Change it to diamonds."

They were playing cards at the Queen's. Donna's idea to avoid doing her English homework. She had snagged Sarah on the street, seen her racing home from the cemetery and convinced her to come hang out. Reluctantly, Sarah had agreed, even though she was secretly grateful. Being with Donna was a relief after the incident at the cemetery. She still hadn't mentioned the photograph; she would wait until the time was right. The extra codeine she had taken was doing its job, too. Making things easier.

Donna abandoned the dictionary and picked up her cards, inspecting them thoughtfully. Shuffling several around, she fanned the cards out neatly, selected one and tossed it onto the pile. "Spades."

Sarah picked a card from the top of the deck, regarded it hopelessly and selected another. Queen of spades. "Pick up five," she said with mild victory, tossing the card to the table.

Donna waved her cigarette dismissively. "I am undaunted." She picked up five cards and threw one down. "Hearts."

"Are you sure?" Sarah asked.

"As sure as death and taxes."

Smiling for the first time, Sarah snapped her cards in a neat row on the table. Three sixes: a heart, a diamond and a club. "Book me out."

Donna threw down her cards, sticking her tongue out in protest. Puffing on her cigarette, she eased back into her seat and stared clinically at Sarah through the smoke. "You look awful," she announced.

Sarah smoothed her hair nervously. "I had a bad night— bad morning, too."

"Maybe you need more rest."

"Yeah, maybe."

"Have you seen Peter lately?"

"Peter?" Sarah asked incredulously. "Why would I see Peter?"

"He's still in love with you, you know."

Sarah bit her tongue to keep from screaming. "It's not my fault, Donna. I've done everything I can to pull away from him without hurting his feelings."

Donna continued to smoke, her silence speaking volumes.

"I can't love him any more. Why can't he accept that?"

"I guess he doesn't want to."

Irritation elbowed Sarah sharply in the ribs. Why should Donna ask her about Peter, anyway? Was this a test, to catch her up, to see how things were going with Michael? Well, two could play that game, she thought. "I always felt you and Peter would make a good couple," she said, manically.

"What? Me?" Donna exclaimed, as if the idea were totally absurd.

"Yeah, you. Come on, you've thought about it," Sarah said, the resentment growing in her voice. "You guys would be great together. You like all the same things. You're physically attracted to each other." She gauged Donna's reaction.

179

"I can't believe you, Sarah," Donna said, grinding her ciga‑
rette into the ashtray. "How's Peter supposed to go out with
me? Not just because he doesn't want to, but because of the
fact that every time he looks at me he thinks of you. How's he
supposed to heal and move on if he just keeps thinking of
you?"

"I really don't care," Sarah snapped back. "Like moths to a
flame, you know?"

"Okay," Donna retorted, visibly hurt. "I just thought you
would like to know."

"I just don't know why *you* care," Sarah continued. "He' a
goof, Donna. I don't know why you won't admit that." She
mimicked Peter, pointing her finger at Donna and shooting
it like a pistol. "Everything that comes out of his mouth is
bullshit."

She reached across the table for the dictionary, thumping
it open to the *B*s. Turning through several pages, she ran her
finger down the column of words. "'Bullshit: taboo slang.
Exaggerated or foolish talk; nonsense.'"

"Okay, fine," Donna conceded angrily.

"'Bogus,'" Sarah barked, flipping several pages back.
"'Spurious or counterfeit; not genuine.'" She pointed her cig‑
arette at Donna. "Admit that he's full of shit."

"I said okay, Wagner," Donna yelled back. "I'm sorry I
brought it up. What is with you these days anyway?"

Sarah clapped the dictionary shut with fierce triumph.
"Like you don't know."

Donna froze in her seat, holding Sarah's poisonous glare
before shifting her eyes to the ashtray. "I didn't mean to hurt
you," she quietly confessed.

"Didn't mean to hurt me?" Sarah seethed, the rage bar‑
relling down on her like a freight train. "What did you mean

to do, then? What could you have possibly meant to achieve by showing me that photo?"

"I don't know," Donna mumbled like a guilty child.

"You may as well have stabbed me with a knife!" Sarah said, her eyes burning with hatred, her cigarette poised, until all at once she crushed the glowing coal into her palm.

"Oh my God!" Donna shouted, jumping up and pulling the cigarette from Sarah's hand.

Slumping over in her seat, anger spent, Sarah stared at her hands in bewilderment. Donna squeezed into the booth beside her, threw her arms around her shoulders.

"I'm sorry, Sarah," she cried, burying her face in Sarah's hair. "I'm so sorry. It's my fault. It's all my fault. I was jealous. I didn't want you to go off with him. I wanted you for myself."

✳   ✳   ✳

Sarah walked up the hill to Michael's, the burn on her hand throbbing, a neat, translucent blister forming where the coal had met her flesh. She'd left Donna back at the Queen's. Insisted on it. Donna hadn't given in easily, begging Sarah to stay with her. Brushing the whole thing off, Sarah had convinced Donna that she was all right. She just needed to be alone, she'd told her. But what she really needed was to see Michael, to feel him next to her. Her body ached to be with him if they were separated too long.

It was the worst part of being in the hospital: the constant fussing without the comfort of human contact. Hands touching without feeling. Performing duties. The needle pricks and examinations pushing the memory of intimacy farther and farther below the skin, until it contracted completely and hid in a secret corner of the subconscious, to be realized only, and tantalizingly, in the liquid world of dreams.

"I can't go home," Sarah announced, standing on the threshold of Michael's house. Michael pushed the door open and took her hand.

"Then don't," he said.

CHAPTER TWELVE

The nausea kicked her awake again. Running to the bathroom, Sarah opened the toilet lid with a crash, only to miss the toilet entirely and vomit on the green-tiled floor. Clinging to the bowl, pyjama knees wet with sick, she waited for the waves of nausea to stop. When the convulsions finally subsided, she dragged herself to her feet, using the towel rack to steady herself. She turned on the tap, and splashed her face, the water cold against her feverish skin, the ends of her long brown hair trailing limply in the sink. She rinsed her mouth too, washing away the acrid taste of vomit, allowing a small amount of water to trickle down her throat and settle in her ravaged stomach.

When she felt sure that she would not be sick again, she turned the water off and dried her face carefully on a towel, removed her pyjama bottoms and discarded them in a rumpled heap in a dry corner of the floor. Using an elastic from her cosmetic bag, she pulled her hair back so that it hung in a loose bun at the nape of her neck, then surveyed the bathroom. The vomit had splashed like watery yellow soup over most of the floor and up one side of the toilet bowl. She was amazed at the amount of it, amazed that it had all come out of her and was now there, on the dingy mint-green tiles.

Reaching under the sink, Sarah pulled out a red bucket with an old rag and filled it with hot water from the tub. She squirted a stream of urine-coloured disinfectant into the steaming water and worked a pair of old orange rubber gloves onto her hands, the damp rubber resisting against her skin. The scent of lemons and antiseptic mingled with the smell of her sick as she began washing the floor. The nausea rose up again and she had to fight the urge to retch, dipping the rag into the scalding water and sloshing it onto the floor and over the toilet, wringing it into the bucket and wiping methodically until everything was clean. Cleaner than it was before. The toilet gurgled and flushed on its own as she poured the grey wash water into the bowl. After rinsing the bucket in the tub, Sarah returned it to its spot under the sink, the rag and gloves draped limply over its side.

In the bedroom, Sarah pushed her dirty pyjamas in a pile beside her dresser. She made her way toward the bed, vertigo almost toppling her as her foot hit something hard and sent it sliding across the floor. It skidded to a stop beside the milk crate. Sarah looked at it warily, the whole room slightly off register. It was *The Book of Living and Dying*. It had lain forgotten beside the dresser since the ritual. Now the pages unfurled to a section on tarot. Suspicious, Sarah hovered over it before picking the book up and crawling into bed. Drifting in and out of consciousness, she trained her eyes on the pages with great effort and found herself reading about the Fool.

He was on a journey. He had met the Magician. But the Magician was a trickster. He knew the answer to the future yet he kept it secret. The Fool continued along the path, meeting the Emperor with all his earthly trappings, and the Lovers in their tentative embrace. The Fool longed to stay with the Lovers but he could not. He had to embark upon a strange course through a desolate land. It was there that he encountered the black-armoured skeleton on a white horse, rising with the sun.

"Rising with the sun." Sarah woke to the sound of her own voice. Forcing herself to stay awake, she began scouring the book for the rest of the story. She had to know what happened to the Fool. But the story simply stopped. The tears welled in her eyes as she stared at the page. Would she ever know the answer to the Fool's riddle?

"Perhaps death is always with us," a sympathetic voice broke through her thoughts, *"as much a part of daily life as the rising sun."*

It was John, sitting on the edge of the bed. Sarah clamped her eyes shut, thought to throw the book at him except that the codeine and her exhaustion wouldn't allow it. Opening her eyes drowsily, she prayed that John would be gone but found him still sitting there. "Please go away," she whispered, as the darkness engulfed her.

* * *

The tree in her dream was getting closer. That she was sure of. There had been times when it seemed just a bush on the horizon, an unidentifiable sort of tree shape off in the distance. But now it stood in front of her, so close she could make out the texture of the bark. The oddest thing about the tree, though, was that it was the only one in the forest that still had all its leaves. She was acutely aware of this and puzzled over the phenomenon even though she knew that she was dreaming. She heard the branches creak as they swayed in time with a faint tune carried on the wind. *Hush, little baby.* The woman began to cry, the light strains of a guitar filtering through her sobs. Sarah reached up to touch one of the leaves but found herself back in bed. Looking up, she saw Peter staring down at her, a bouquet of orange chrysanthemums in one hand. He smiled, holding a finger to his lips.

"How did you get in here?" she asked.

He shook his head mutely.

"You have to leave," she ordered. She reached for the light but he stopped her midway with his hand.

Placing the flowers beside the bed, he began pulling his shirt over his head. Sarah watched as he stripped down to his socks, his body lean and muscular. He lifted one edge of the covers to climb in next to her.

"The socks," she said, pointing to his feet.

He peeled them off and crept stealthily into the bed. Retrieving the flowers, he rubbed them playfully under her chin then discarded them to one side and began tugging on the ties of her gown. Sarah fumbled obediently with the ties even though she didn't really want to be with Peter. She was Michael's girl now. But Peter was so persistent. And she felt guilty for the love she couldn't return. *One last time, to say goodbye,* she told herself as she pulled the gown up to her shoulders and worked it over her head. He coaxed it the rest of way, tossing it wantonly across the room so that it drooped like an exhausted ghost in one corner. For some reason this made her giggle. Peter found her mouth in the darkness and kissed her hard, his breathing heavy with passion. He moved so that he was on top of her, the bedsprings creaking in protest, the bouquet of orange chrysanthemums tumbling recklessly to the floor.

* * *

Sarah couldn't breathe. His hands gripped her throat, squeezing. She clawed at his face, her lips turning purple, then blue, eyes bulging, his hands pressing with increasing force until the strength left her and she could do little more than batter listlessly at the air. *He's killing me,* she thought, as she burst into consciousness to find him sitting calmly next to her on the bed. She couldn't move, couldn't scream, couldn't avert her eyes, or demand to know what he wanted. She just prayed silently to God to save her, to take him away. And John magically complied, getting up from the side of the bed and leaving the room.

* * *

There was something knocking in the house. She was sure it was him, trying to get in. But it was only Donna, tapping on the bedroom window, her earnest face pressed against the glass.

"Sarah. It's Donna."

Sarah sat up, the pain mushrooming in her head.

"Open the window," Donna said. She helped from the other side as Sarah reached clumsily across the bed and forced the window up.

"What are you doing here?" she mumbled. "It's freezing out."

"Come to the Queen's with me."

Sarah stared blankly back at her. She wanted to go to Michael's. But he was busy, working on his secret project. "Give me a minute," she said. "I'll meet you out front."

The window rattled shut and Donna disappeared from the frame. Sarah rubbed her face with her hands and got up from bed. Plucking a pair of blue dress socks from the pile of dirty laundry, she sat on the bed, crossing one leg over the other, her bare foot stuck in the air to receive the sock. It looked odd to see her foot like that—suddenly exposed—like his feet.

Sprouting out from beneath the sheets like old turnips. Yellowed. The nails hard and overgrown. Seemingly detached, as if placed there for a gag. It took several rounds with the nail clippers to tame those nails, the clippings firing wildly across the room. And the lotion. Gallons of scented emollient applied by the hour to the gentle hum of a lullaby. Hands folding and unfolding like a dove's wings, taking special care over the birthmark on the left ankle, a butterfly-shaped bloodstain.

It wasn't right for the living to be obsessed with the dead, Sarah concluded disdainfully, working the socks over her feet, then leaning drunkenly on the bed, drained from the effort. She reached down and recovered her jeans, inching them slowly up her legs and over her hips, past the oak tree tattoo. Pulling an old sweatshirt over her head, she didn't even bother checking her face in the mirror or brushing her teeth before shuffling into the hall for her boots and coat.

The expression on Donna's face when Sarah emerged from the house caused her to search her purse for her compact. Looking in the small round mirror, she laughed softly at her own indifference.

"Don't worry about it," Donna reassured her. "You look like you know all the right people, if you know what I mean..."

At the Queen's, Sarah chose their usual booth at the back of the shop, away from the other students. Donna ordered fries and coffee. Sarah ordered tea. She noticed that Donna didn't smoke. Didn't even pull out her Zippo the way she normally would. She caught Donna's eyes flickering over the burn on her hand. Unspoken concern. They sipped their drinks self-consciously, trying to ignore the uncomfortable silence.

"I found footprints by the bed," Sarah finally said. She took the bottle of codeine from her purse and swished a couple tablets back with a gulp of tea.

Donna's cup stopped midway to her lips, her gaze shifting momentarily to the near-empty bottle of codeine.

"That's how I knew he came into my room," Sarah continued.

Donna nodded, her face blank.

She doesn't believe me, Sarah thought. "He took the knife, too," she persevered. "I'm sure of it."

"What knife?"

"The one I took to bed with me."

Donna seemed to ponder this for a moment, then started in about malevolent ghosts. Hadn't Sarah seen *The Haunting*, or *The Woman in Black*? Some ghosts attach themselves to one person in particular and make it their business to haunt that person to the end of their days.

Make it their business. Sarah found something amusing

189

in that, in the face of everything. The business of ghosts. Even in death, the drive to pursue a higher purpose. No malingering for you, ghosts. Get off your spectral duffs and make a name for yourself! Sarah laughed out loud.

"Poltergeists," Donna persisted. "Sometimes they'll even follow you if you move away, so there's no sense trying to outsmart them. They'll find you, no matter where you go."

No. Not poltergeists. John was definitely not malevolent—at least, not outside her dreams. And the others, the girl and the crying woman. They didn't seem angry or violent either. They just seemed to want to reach her, to tell her something. Something she couldn't understand or decipher.

"Even Houdini couldn't find his way back from the dead," she said.

Donna looked confused. "Did he want to?"

"Yes, he wanted to." Sarah leaned to one side of the booth. "He thought he could come back from the dead. It was a quest for truth."

"Is that why he was always jumping off the Harvard Bridge?"

Sarah sighed. She was wasting her time. Donna didn't really understand anything out of the ordinary, for all her professed interest in such things. Who was she, anyway? With her messy hair and her black-rimmed eyes? Even now, looking at her across the table, Sarah saw in Donna's face the image of many young women, merging together, protean. At times distinct, familiar; at times blurred, as though suspended at the bottom of a swimming pool, her features wavering with the sunlight and wind over the water. Is that how it had been for him? Sarah wondered.

The nurses' faces one in the same, their bodies coalescing,
individual traits erased by the longing for one thing. Mor-
phine. That generous, ephemeral god, carried on the wings of
a white-sneakered and temperamental angel.

Sarah felt suddenly put out. She wouldn't even have been
at the Queen's if Michael hadn't been busy working on the
secret project he refused to tell her about. But she had a
project of her own. A plan she'd been hatching for a while.
And she needed his help.

"I have to go," she said.

❊   ❊   ❊

Sarah picked her way through the woods, Michael in tow.
He carried John's guitar. There was a calm in the air, an
immaculate stillness. Sarah stepped over a thick tree root
that pushed up through the path like a gnarled hand. "I'm
sorry, what did you say?" she asked.

"Frost," Michael said.

She nodded distractedly, her breathing laboured from the
effort of walking. "Yeah, it's cold."

"Him," Michael said, pointedly. "I was quoting the poet.
'The woods are lovely, dark and deep.'"

"Oh, right."

"Are you sure you want to do this?" He gestured toward
the guitar.

"Yes. I'm sure."

"I'm just afraid you may regret it."

"I don't have a choice," she said with unprovoked irritation. "I can't think of any other reason why he keeps coming back."

Michael placed a hand on her shoulder. "Hey, I'm trying to help."

Sarah hung her head. "I know. But I have to try something." She wrung her pale hands together as she walked off the path into the woods. "Over here," she said standing before a large, rough-looking trunk. "This is an oak. A white oak. The tree in my dream is like this one."

As she spoke these words, a large buck appeared from behind the tree, regarded them, then stepped majestically into the forest and was gone.

It's a sign, Sarah thought, kneeling slowly in front of the tree. "We'll leave it here."

Placing the guitar at the foot of the oak, Michael sprinkled the ground with flakes of tobacco from the leather pouch that he'd pulled from his coat pocket.

"I divest myself," Sarah murmured, touching the guitar repeatedly. *That should do it,* she said to herself. *That should help.*

Michael held her tightly as they left, leaving the guitar at the base of the tree. In silence, they moved to the open field of the park, working their way along the low buildings and empty birdcages, navigating toward the boathouse, its doors and windows boarded up. As they walked past the boathouse, Sarah heard a sound.

"What is that?" she asked.

"What?"

"That strange scratching noise . . . listen." She cocked her head to one side. "It sounds like it's coming from the boathouse." She scanned the building. The scratching grew louder, followed by the sound of broken fluttering. "There!"

she exclaimed, pointing to a window near the top of the building where a board was missing, revealing broken glass and wire mesh, a large gap at the top of the frame. The bird lay collapsed at the bottom of the window, pale blue feathers blowing delicately through the wire, like flower petals in the wind. "It's a pigeon or something, trapped in the window."

Michael moved to take a better look. The bird flapped mechanically, its long thin beak speared through a hole in the mesh, its wings folded awkwardly in the small space. "It's not a pigeon," he said. "It's a kingfisher."

"Oh, Michael, do something!" Sarah cried.

Standing on tiptoe, Michael reached toward the window, the bird flapping against the glass in violent bursts. "It's too high."

"We have to help it!" Sarah said, her voice breaking. "We have to get it out of there!"

Michael gestured to a small house across the park. "That building . . . there's supposed to be a caretaker there."

Sarah ran toward the house, Michael beside her. Tripping up the stairs, she opened the door and rushed into an empty room. "Hello? Is anyone here?"

A gruff-looking man appeared through a doorway at the back, wiping his hands on an old rag. "Can I help you?"

"There's a bird trapped in the boathouse," Sarah breathlessly explained. "A kingfisher. We have to save it."

The man surveyed her coldly, continuing to wipe his hands.

"We have to get it out!" Sarah insisted. "We can't leave it there. It'll die!"

"Probably half dead already," the man said.

"Look, have you got a ladder or something?" Michael interjected. "I can't reach that bird without one."

"Sure, sure." The man sauntered back through the door and returned moments later, carrying a metal stepladder.

Taking the ladder, Michael lifted it easily through the door and down the stairs, Sarah trotting behind him, the man watching indifferently through the window at the door. When they reached the boathouse, Michael popped the ladder open. Sarah braced it on either side with her hands as he climbed up.

"I don't know how a kingfisher got stuck here," he said. "I thought they migrated."

"Hurry Michael," Sarah begged, clinging to the ladder as it listed to one side with his weight.

The bird scrabbled to get away, one wild yellow eye glinting as Michael struggled to loosen the mesh. "It's no good," he said. "We need a hammer . . . or a set of pliers or something. I'll have to ask that man."

Sarah was nearly beside herself with anguish by the time Michael reappeared from the house, running, pliers and hammer in hand. He skipped up the ladder and began working at the corner of the mesh with the claw of the hammer. Staples pinged through the air as Michael pulled the wire up, curling it forward. He reached his hand in, fingers outstretched, the bird flapping frantically before it collapsed.

"You've killed it," a contemptuous voice proclaimed.

It was the caretaker, standing behind them, a supercilious smile across his face. Michael pushed his arm in farther, the wire pressing against the crux of his elbow. Folding his hand delicately over the back of the bird, he pulled it carefully along the glass to the opening, eased the bird free and released it.

Sarah swooned as the kingfisher fell lifeless toward the ground, until suddenly, in a burst of instinct greater than fear, its wings shot out like switchblades at its sides, slicing the air, lifting it over the trees, across the glistening pond and down the slate-coloured river. They watched as the bird contracted to a tiny speck in the winter sky.

Michael turned, flattened the wire against the window frame with a few good hits of the hammer and climbed down the ladder. Resting the tools on one of the rungs, he reached out to Sarah. She collapsed in his arms, sobbing against his chest, her body shaking, the taste of wool and tears in her mouth. He held her until her body was still, then lifted her face with his hand. The man watched as Michael brushed the hair from her lips and eyes, kissing her devotedly. Without a word, Michael wrapped his arm around Sarah's shoulders and began guiding her across the parking lot, their bodies falling in rhythm, their feet matching steps.

When they reached the house, Michael helped her to the front door. He worked the key in the lock with one hand, holding Sarah firmly with the other as though he were afraid she would disappear should he let go. She clung to him with equal need as he pushed the door open and ushered her into the house. Using the ball of his foot to help secure the latch in the jamb, he closed the door against the cold. They moved to his room as a single unit and stood before the bed. Her hair danced with static as he removed the knit cap from her head and unwound her scarf. Fingers trembling, she fumbled with the smooth machined plastic of his coat buttons. They bent down together in a mirrored dance, knees touching as they reached the buttons at the bottom of each other's coats, pushing the shoulders down, the coats sliding off in two dark heaps like lifeless skins against the floor. They moved to the bed, his mouth on hers, his hands working the buttons on her blouse. Placing her hand to his mouth, she kissed his lips between her fingers. He pulled her down on the bed, sliding her blouse over her shoulders and wrists, dropping it to the floor beside the coats, their bodies mingling at last in a tangle of skin and hair.

CHAPTER THIRTEEN

The secret project was finally out of the bag. Michael had animated the girl, in the same way he had given life to the images of John. "I wanted it to be a surprise," he said. And it was, especially since he had given the girl Sarah's face.

"It's not really your face," he explained. "I blurred the corners. You have to look at it very closely to know that it's you."

It frightened Sarah to see the diaphanous image of herself moving through the cyber-forest Michael had created, floating up to the oak tree, turning, waving invitingly.

"What does it prove?"

"Nothing," he said, "But maybe you can lay the whole thing to rest, now that the girl has a context."

"But it didn't work for John," Sarah said. "It just made matters worse. Everything's falling apart. The girl—I dream about her all the time now. And the woman crying, it sounds as if she's right beside me. I can't sleep at night any more, no matter how much medication I take. Just look at me!" She spun around to face him. "I'm a wreck. Can't you see that? I'm a horrible wreck!" She folded in a sobbing heap to the floor.

Michael ran to her, helped her to the bed. He laid her down, pulled the covers up and over her shoulders, tucking them in around her. "Rest."

* * *

Sarah stared glumly out the window. In her hand she held a note from the school, on official letterhead, requesting an explanation for the days she had missed: seventeen and a half. She wondered briefly what constituted the half day as the letter dropped listlessly from her hand, tracing gentle arcs to the floor. She turned her attention back to the view in her window. The birds filled the tree branches—house sparrows—trilling courageously against the cold. Chirping. Twittering. These were not happy sounds. They made her think of spring, the urgent singing, heralding the beginning of another mating cycle. More birds fighting for the right to breed. More nests built. More eggs laid. More chicks to hatch and screech for food, only to be blown out of the trees at the faintest hint of wind, too young to fly. It happened every spring. The starlings were the worst, their numbers legion to beat the cruelty of nature's odds. And so, come April, the sidewalks would be littered with fledglings, hop-hop-hopping innocently along, their parents calling out encouragement from the trees and telephone wires. Every moment outside would be spent herding the little birds off the road and onto the grass, only to hear their pitiful squawks as they eventually succumbed to neighbourhood cats. Later, out walking, she would find a half-feathered wing on the sidewalk, or a tiny leg, a tuft of down still attached at the top.

It was fitting, though, that so much death be associated with so much life. Some must go so that others may come—that's what the little birds had taught her.

There was a problem with the intravenous. The veins, over months of abuse, had collapsed. Arms like deflated inner tubes. Patched and gaunt. The skin withered, wrinkled, like old plums. The nurses poked and poked, a macabre quilting bee, the needle stabbing through the skin and out the other side.

"What in God's name is going on here?" the doctor demanded.

A call was put in to the expert. She arrived, neat and pressed as a cotton blouse from the cleaners, knelt beside the bed, her kit at her feet. She stroked the molested arm sorrowfully, tenderly as a flower petal. Inspected the punctures and bruises. Ran a finger down the dry riverbeds of empty veins. Her silver needle found the hidden spring on first attempt, the quick drip, drip, drip of intravenous solution, until the plastic wheel was rolled back along the tube to stay the flow.

A meeting was called. The staff depended upon meetings. It was determined that the hospital was no longer needed. Home care would ease the emotional burden, they said. And the burden on the taxpayer's dollar. There was no real treatment required. Only maintenance. Morphine and saline. The sickness was too far gone for much else. But then the fever arrived almost as if to say, "See? Committees can't predict everything." The file was stamped "pending."

❊   ❊   ❊

It was in the shower that Sarah discovered the stain on her ankle. Lathering her leg with soap, she scrubbed at it with a sponge. But as the suds swirled down the drain, she could see that the mark was still there. A wine-red stain, like a butterfly. She couldn't reconcile it being there, so she ignored it. Although later, as she dressed, she couldn't help but glance down and acknowledge it, a dull red Rorschach blot.

As she stumbled toward sleep that night, the codeine pushing her down the hill toward unconsciousness, she met the woman's cries pushing their way up. Sarah could see the girl, too, waiting for her in the shadows. With great effort she forced her mind to turn around, sent it scrabbling back up the hill again and into the light where the trap door waited for her.

She crawled out of bed and with much effort inched one of the boxes from the little closet in her room over the blue-and-green rug to secure the door.

*　*　*

Sarah clutched the sheets on the bed, eyes rolling. *Was she dreaming or awake?* She could not move, her body as heavy as wet concrete oozing into the mattress. Her tongue worked in the dry cave of her mouth, searching for the edges of words, twisting helplessly like a sticky red slug. With the force of great willpower, she inched her hand, painfully, deliberately, to the side of the bed, worked her fingers over the mattress and down to the cold metal frame to trace the letters engraved there: *T.G.H.* John appeared, hovering in the doorway. He glided into the room, opened the codeine bottle and extracted three tablets, pushing them one after the other between her parched lips, then watched as she lay there, waiting, the bitter tablets dissolving slowly in her mouth.

※　※　※

There were five boxes over the trap door now. They made Sarah feel better about the nightly traffic in her room, even though the boxes hadn't stopped anything. The footsteps, the voices whispering. Sometimes she would sit in the dark with the hope of catching them, bolting upright in bed, snapping the light on furiously. Or she would doze, eyes half open, hoping to trick them into showing themselves.

The girl was getting bolder too. In a voice distant and ethereal, she started calling Sarah's name. Sarah struggled to move her feet, terrified should the girl lure her successfully to the tree—yet desperate to reach it all the same. And the tree itself had started changing, seeming to come to life through the girl, embodying her desire and intent. It transmogrified to deceive Sarah, the leaves shimmering gold, then silver, the bark glinting like cut glass, then milky and smooth as porcelain. Sarah tried to fool it, tried to break its hold on her by slashing the tree on her hip with a razor blade, the blood blossoming like strange red fruit from its inky green branches.

And then the phone, ringing. She thought not to pick it up, but for some reason couldn't stop herself and did. She heard the ambient buzz in the background as she slowly lowered the handset to the cradle, a woman's voice calling out repeatedly over the wire. *"Hello? Hello?"* It was the girl. Sarah was sure of it.

When John appeared next, Sarah was shocked to discover him sitting in the middle of the bed holding her hand. She buried her face in her pillow until she was sure he was gone. When she finally raised her head, she was incensed to find her mother, dour, pitiful, sitting where John had been. She wanted to shout for her to leave, to get out of the room. But the codeine was in control, stealing the words like a soft-shoed thief from her mouth. Because it was all she could do, she turned her head from her mother in wordless protest, the way he had done.

Blankets moulded over the body, skin bleached white as sheets. Eyes closed. Mind reeling. Silence occupying the rightful place of voiced rage, the passive demonstration ultimately, disappointingly impotent.

Alone, Sarah forced herself to get out of bed. Teetering on unsure legs like a newborn calf, she worked her way to the door in stages: leaning on the side of the bed, clinging to the edge of the dresser, grappling for the door handle.

In the bathroom she grasped the rim of the sink, staring at the stranger facing her in the mirror. Sunken cheekbones, eyes ringed with fatigue. Hair dull and lifeless, coming away in her hands. Wiggling her fingers over the garbage can, she watched as the hair floated down, light as a prayer into the trash.

Coming off onto the pillow in a kind of nuclear-blast shadow of the head

The nightgown was stubborn, catching at her wrists and her chin. She caught her breath and tugged, dropping the gown to the floor. The lip of the tub cut into the back of her legs as she perched there, marvelling at the size of her kneecaps beneath the thin veil of skin. Leaning forward, she allowed herself to slide into the tub. She worked the taps, turning them by squeaking inches, the water trickling from the spout and eventually gushing into the bottom of the tub, swirling around her feet and buttocks. Engaging the shower lever, she wrapped her arms around her legs and let the water spray over her shoulders and back. She would go to see Michael, she thought. She would tell him about her knees.

✻   ✻   ✻

The walk to Michael's seemed to take forever. Her feet were leaden, her head dizzy and light as her mind ricocheted erratically, back and forth and sideways. The streets and houses, the trees and sidewalk, everything was slightly skewed. Resting on the bridge, she could see her secret spot down on the tracks. And there, beside the boxcar. Who was it? The old man from the cemetery. *Mr. Ellis from 317.* Their eyes met. Sarah pushed away from the wall, continued along the bridge. Feet moving step over step. Heavy as cannon-balls. At the grove of pine trees she stopped. Had to stop. Stooping over, hands braced on her thighs. She glanced over her shoulder, expecting the man to appear behind her.

But, no, she was alone. She straightened herself and began toiling across the stretch of ground to the parking lot. A plaintive cry echoed across the stillness of the park. *The woman.* Sarah listened. It was a peacock, calling from inside its cage. Plumage painted and gleaming like a Japanese kimono, the peacock paraded regally along the length of fence. Sarah took a moment to admire it. It was the first time she'd seen one in the park. The bird cocked its luminous head and watched as Sarah made her way across the parking lot, calling woefully after her as she set out up the hill.

At his house, the windows were dark.

The curtains drawn, preventing the light from coming in

Clutching the ledge, she balanced tiptoe on the rock and peered through his bedroom window. When she couldn't see him, she walked around to the front of the house and attempted the door. It was unlocked and slightly ajar. She pushed it lightly, the door creaking slowly open. "Michael?"

Mouth shaping words without meaning, the mechanical wails from some primitive place deep inside as the body began to expire

Stepping tentatively over the threshold, Sarah called out again. "Michael?" The door to his room was open. She took a few halting steps down the hall and stood in the doorway.

Where the nurses had nervously collected, while others trotted purposefully down the corridor

The room no longer neat but messy, as though he'd been looking for something in a hurry. Sarah sat down on the bed.

She was so tired. She needed to rest. She lowered herself slowly onto the comforter, the pillow cool against her cheek. Pulling her feet up, she curled into a little ball. She would stay like this for a while and wait.

The family gathering around the bed, weeping, confused faces searching for answers that were not there, labouring through the minutes, desperate for a peaceful resolution

But by morning when he had not arrived, she began to grow restless. She rose from the bed. The videos were in a heap on the floor. There was one beside the TV. A new one. An image of Michael and Donna flickered distantly through her mind.

The sudden kick of memory asserting itself, of life resisting surrender

Sarah turned on the TV, took the cassette from its case and pushed it into the VCR. The screen buzzed. The image grew clear. It was Sarah as a little girl, playing in her bikini in the plastic pool. She looked up at her brother and laughed, splashing him with water.

The intravenous dripping slower and slower

To one side, her mother, mouthing instructions from a patio chair, hair in curlers. Sarah watched with wonder as John jumped in and out of the pool, kicking water into the air. The scene faded and changed. It was Christmas.

The chance for miracles quickly unravelling

She was there, tearing open a package, pulling a doll from inside. She held it up to the camera, hugging it over and over with delight. John walked into the frame, cowboy hat tilted to one side. Lining himself up, he pulled a pistol from his holster and shot something off screen.

A thin trail of blood emerging from one nostril, eyelashes fluttering, chest heaving

The picture faded to black, then emerged again. It was her mother and father, young, smiling. They held a baby in their arms. They cooed and clucked over the infant, kissing its head and face with pride.

Arms enfolding, voices strained to the point of breaking, lips held closely to the ear, speaking through the moans

That she should find this filled her with awe and confusion. She watched the video for what seemed like hours, her face shining with tears as her life unfolded in front of her, through infancy to young adulthood, the shy joy of her first ballet recital to the anguish of skinned knees and broken hearts. She could not imagine how Michael had managed to create it.

An entire life playing out to its inevitable conclusion, the momentary glimmers of recognition, fingers working the air

As the last images faded and crackled from view, Sarah turned off the TV. The room was quiet and dark. Michael had not come home. She stared at the blank screen, knew that if she was going to understand any of it, she would have to see the old woman again. Walking from the room, her heart resonated with the one truth that the video had imparted, the extraordinary message that Michael had so carefully pieced together in the hundreds of ordinary little scenes held there.

"I love you."

*   *   *

The train trundled along the tracks. It swayed and rocked like a willow tree, urging her to sleep. Outside, the rain poured down, lashing against the windows and making it impossible to see. Inside, a few lone riders sat stiffly in their seats. Sarah recognized the old man's hat, and the little boy from Michael's videos, too. She slouched down to avoid eye contact when the old man turned to look at her. So she could stretch out her feet, she raised the armrest of the seat next to her, then covered her legs with her jacket and rested, the bundle of pictures clasped in her hand. The movement of the train lulled her, the whistle blowing mournfully in the distance, the engine hundreds of feet ahead down the tracks. The train was picking up speed as it left the city, careening through the night toward Salem. It wouldn't be a long ride. Just enough to get some rest.

Sarah woke as the train slowed to a crawl and lurched to a stop at the station. There was the clamour and bang as the stairs unfolded to the platform. She sat up and looked around. The train was empty, save for herself. She wondered briefly where the other people had gone. Her jacket dropped lifelessly to the floor as she got up and made her way along the aisle to the door. The door was open, the stairs waiting. She stepped carefully down, photos in one hand, holding the rail with the other for support. The rain had stopped; the station was deserted. She had to jump down from the last step, the conductor graciously assisting her. The train bucked forward, and the conductor disappeared inside the car as Sarah walked toward the stairs that led to the street. They were long and steep, switching back several flights; the rubber soles of her sneakers struck bluntly against the metal treads.

As she neared the top, Sarah could see that the streets were also empty. Stopping at a crosswalk, she waited dutifully for the light to blink from red to green, then crossed into the town square. The shops were closed, their windows uninviting and dark. Walking past the familiar rows of red-brick buildings, Sarah searched for the alley. When it didn't present itself she began to worry that she had the wrong street, that she'd remembered it incorrectly. But it soon came into view, a gap between two buildings. Sarah stood at the mouth of it, the alley stretching into the shadows. There was a small white light at the end, illuminating the way.

She stepped into the alley. She hardly knew what she would say to the old woman when she saw her. Her footsteps echoed softly against the buildings as she walked, counting out the numbers as she went: 15, 17, 19. Where was 17½? She turned, retraced her steps. She could not find the door. *Where was it?*

Sarah lowered herself against the wall in defeat. She looked at the bundle of photos in her hand. They were all out of order. Who had done that? From somewhere in the alley, the cries of the woman began to filter through the darkness. Sarah buried her face in her hands, the photos fluttering to the ground at her feet. She began to weep, in deep sobs that shook her body to its frame. She wept for her mother and her father and for John. She wept for Michael and Donna and Peter. And for all the people she had known and would never know. She wept for life, with all its beautiful intricacies, and for death, in all its mystery. Most of all she wept for the Fool, travelling alone and without direction in a desolate land. *Silly little fool.* She saw the faces of the masks around her, laughing, scowling, muttering prayers. She wept until she heard a soothing voice calling her name.

"Sarah. Sarah."

It was Michael, standing in the alley.

"The Fool," Sarah cried, her body wracked with sobs. "He meets a skeleton in black armour upon a white horse . . ."

". . . Rising with the sun," Michael said, completing her thought. He walked toward her, his voice steady and calm. "He knows that he is in the presence of Death. He fears for his own life and for the lives of those he loves. He thinks to flee, but knows in the vast stretch of barren land that he cannot possibly outrun Death, and so, faces him."

"'Am I dead?'" the Fool asks.

"'You have left all you know behind,' Death answers. 'But this is not the end. It is but a new beginning. A transformation.'"

Michael reached for Sarah's hands, pulling her gently to her feet. She clung to him like a newborn, her mind a pinwheel of questions as they moved to the end of the alley, where the bricks gave way to soil and the town fell away to trees. The light in the alley burst, illuminating the way along the path that curved and snaked through the woods, a ribbon of moonlight in the dark, though there was no moon in the sky. Her breath rattled, as if her lungs were filling with water instead of air, inhaling and exhaling in rhythm with Michael's own; her body, heavy as clay.

"I'm so scared," she said.

Michael squeezed her shoulders. They were walking toward the oak tree, the same one from her dream. Turning to face Michael, Sarah was met by her own countenance peering curiously back at her. It was the girl. She was the girl. Michael had been right about that. The cries of the woman rose up, filling the air before fading to the faintest mewling. And there was something else there. Another voice. John's voice.

"Sarah . . . Sarah, I love you."

Sarah laughed and lowered her eyes. She was surprised to find her blue sock feet outlined sharply against the earth. Had she forgotten to put her shoes on? Pulling off the socks, she began removing the rest of her clothes, scattering them carelessly along the path as she walked. She felt so free. Her naked body shimmered with a sparkling translucence. As she gazed at it in wonder, she understood at last. There was nothing left to fear. She moved toward the tree, its branches reaching out to her, a single exquisite leaf escaping and falling in gentle arcs to the ground. From somewhere far off in the distance, she heard the sound of a door quietly closing. The heaviness left her body and she began to rise toward the sky, like the kingfisher with wings like knives, up, up, into a pool of silver light.

*　*　*

Sarah lay on the bed, eyelids fluttering like pale butterflies, mouth gaping, her body shuddering with the memory of life. Mrs. Wagner clasped her daughter's frail hand, her cries spilling over into the hallway and down to the nurses' station. Cradling the pillow behind Sarah's head, John supported her small frame until the convulsions finally stopped. He held her as the sun slowly blossomed in the window, and a street lamp burst, spreading phosphorous seeds over the sidewalk. When he was sure that it was finished, John eased himself free, careful not to jostle the body. Sitting delicately at the foot of the bed, he wept, a dry, fathomless grief beyond tears.

The nurses lurked outside the door of the room, hands in pockets, faces etched with rehearsed concern. It was a shame, they all agreed, to see this happen to someone so young. Breaching the sanctity of sorrow, Dr. Field offered condolences to the family, speaking haltingly about the afterlife and what natives believe happens in death, causing everyone to feel awkward, including himself, until he relented and left the room, bumping the bedside table clumsily and knocking a blue glass tumbler to the floor with an astonishing crash.

* * *

Beneath the oldest oak tree in the Terrace cemetery there stands a stone. It is black granite and almost always decorated with fresh flowers or pine cone offerings. There are words engraved there, under the thinnest crescent of moon. *"One under heaven."* And in its corner, a small porcelain picture of the girl, shaped in a neat oval, the suggestion of a smile on her lips—a Mona Lisa smile—as though she guards a secret that she will never tell. Perhaps she was amused by the words of the priest who boomed with breaking emotion, *"Who knows but life be that which men call death, and death what men call life?"* Or by the size of the funeral, the students pouring out the doors of the church when the pews were full. People paying their respects. Family. Teachers. Boys and girls that she had known and would never know. Hands in pockets, staring vacantly, absorbed with the notion of lives lived and lost. The impossible fabric of living and dying, the weft and warp of individual experience, strung out on the fragile loom of the human mind. The constant niggling of "what if"s.

Or perhaps it was the snow appearing magically after the rain, falling gently at first then whirling through the air, great deific shears snipping away at so much lace. And at the cemetery, the trees sighing in the emptiness, the absence of everything, even ghosts. But in the spring, through the urgent chatter of birds, the delicate mauve prayers of the crocus rise up, and later, the bright faces of forget-me-nots.

ACKNOWLEDGEMENTS

Sincere thanks and appreciation to the gang at Harper-Collins Canada, especially Lynne Missen, Akka Janssen and Katie Hearn. Hearty thanks to the math people at Dr. Math for all their good advice. A huge salute and great admiration to Michio Takagi for his artistic stylings and tech wizardry. Warmest thanks to Laura Taylor for her talents and friendship, and to the Dixits for their kindness over the years. Gros becs to Lucie Pagé, the Francophone Goddess. Profound love and deepest gratitude to Wesley and Brian for their unwavering faith, and to my whole family for their enduring support: Mum, Mark, Rita, Cindy, Monika, Norman, Cassel, Hayden, Jasmine, Charlene and Jim. Hats off to Dom and Cath—same time next year? Thanks to Naomi and Doug for knowing what it's all about, and to Marilyn and Ade. And special thanks to Chris and Richard for caring enough to share in this wild journey.